FATHOMS BELOW

A Short Story Bundle Drenched with Romance

AVA CUVAY

Under the sea, Atlantia's mer-creatures are devoting full time to floating... and falling in love.

"Fathoms Below"

written by Ava Cuvay

Copyright ©2025

Published by Drinking the Stars Press, LLC

P.O. Box 32, Whitestown, IN 46075

Cover Design by Emily Hailey

ISBN 979-8-9991313-0-0 (print)

ISBN 979-8-9991313-1-7 (digital)

Website: AvaCuvay.com

Facebook Page: AvaCuvayAuthor

DEDICATION

To all the mermaids out there, everyone who loves making waves, and those who find calm in the ebb and flow of the tides. May the waters be always warm and the currents always at your back.

BETTER WHERE IT'S WETTER

Ariel LaRue assumes the sexy merman pictured on the lake house is "just art." Then a violent storm topples her into his arms, and she discovers the ocean isn't the only thing that gets her wet.

"Are you a mermaid?"

The child's question pulled me from the nap I'd drifted into. The gentle waves of Lake Triton, one of the largest luxury gated water communities here on Aquata Prime, had lured me away from my paintings to come play. Instead, I'd fallen asleep on my inflatable raft in the warmth of the late afternoon sun, dreams of fanciful sea creatures swimming in my head. I was tempted to blame the vivid imaginings on my solitude these past few weeks—housesitting out here on the lake didn't always suit social people like me—but I wasn't lonely, and I wasn't alone. I had my painting supplies to keep me occupied. And the picture of a handsome merman on the wall to keep me company.

I lowered my sunglasses to peer at the little girl standing at the stern of the boat sliding silently through the water. I hadn't heard the boat approach, yet it was already docking against the side of the floating house I currently called home. The girl was young, perhaps five, with a fuzzy halo of red curls, her brown eyes bright with wonder. She leaned so far forward, I feared she might tumble from the low bow into the water.

She thought I was a mermaid? That would be a childhood dream-come-true, if such were possible. I returned her smile. "What makes you think I'm a mermaid, sweetie?"

"You have a green tail and your hair is my favorite color!"

Her confident tone implied I should be well aware of the requirements for being a mermaid. My gaze followed where she pointed to my legs. Sure enough, the emerald-green wrap I'd worn in my customary attempt to hide my thighs had slipped and now trailed in the water like a broad tail making lazy circles in the water. Top that with my elbow-length curls dyed *flamingo pink*, and I made an adequate impersonation of what a little girl might imagine a mermaid to be.

"Oh, I can't be a mermaid." There weren't any seashells in all the waters of Aquata Prime big enough to cover my large buoys. My ample cleavage was often a hassle—like whenever I jogged or slept on my stomach or stood upright—but she didn't need to know that. I stuck my bottom lip out in an exaggerated pout. "Mermaids are notoriously beautiful singers, and I can't hold a tune to save my life."

I warbled a few off-key notes. She covered her mouth and giggled. I laughed with her.

The boat slid flush with the dock and a middle-aged woman with a more sedate version of the girl's hair stood from the captain's seat. She nodded a friendly greeting. "You must be the house sitter for the Morays. The one from the artist colony?"

I swung my legs over the side of my float to sit up. "Yes, I'm Ariel LaRue. You're Eartha from the Farmer's Market, right? The Morays said you'd be by."

"Yep, and this is my daughter, Terra. We usually swing through every few weeks with groceries or anything else you might need. 'Course the water taxis can be called if you want something immediately or are dying to walk on dry land for a bit."

Aquata Prime was a planet of water dotted with a few strips of land crowded with towering cities such as the one I'd grown up in. Urban megaliths filled with noise and chaos and crappy boyfriends. The thought of leaving Lake Triton before I'd soaked up every last possible bit of peace and quiet made me laugh. "Thanks, but water is my Zen Garden. I went through six interviews and sat on a three-year waiting list to get a dream job like this. My toes aren't touching land until they absolutely have to."

"I know what you mean. A bad day on the water is still better than a good day on land." Eartha laughed with me. "I assume the Morays left you pretty well stocked. Anything they missed?"

I looked at the lake house behind me, a two-story floating mansion in the middle of a lake the size of our smallest moon. This model of luxury and wealth—I wouldn't have cared if it were a raft of driftwood bound with twine—would be my home for the next few months while the owners vacationed on a nearby planet. Skiing. In snow. I shuddered. Precipitation should only come in its liquid form, if anyone cared to know my opinion on the matter.

"I'm well stocked with food. But I'd love some fresh sushi." As I expected, Eartha shook her head.

"Sorry hon. We only have hydroponic offerings. You're on your own for fish." She chuckled when I grimaced at the thought of catching and cleaning my own fish. I could barely catch a man worth the time it took to enjoy dinner. Sushi would have to wait.

Eartha nodded toward the south. "Weather shows a big storm coming. Waves could get ugly so you might want to submerge tonight."

I'd seen the reports as well, but her advice reminded me of another issue. "Would you happen to know of a handyman? The door to the mechanical room won't stay closed and the noise is distracting. Plus, I'm pretty sure that's a code violation. But Woody from the community's office is busy."

She shook her head again. "Sorry, can't help you there either. The lake community manager might have been able to fix it, but no one's seen him for a few months. He up and disappeared one day and no one's heard a peep from him. Not even his family. That leaves Woody until they can hire another, and he's got his hands full with the Fischer's place. Their bladder has a leak."

A bladder leak was serious. These lake houses were built to withstand category ten hurricanes, but not the depths to which a house would sink without a functioning bladder. My gut churned for their predicament. "My door can wait. I hope he gets the Fischer's fixed in time."

Eartha nodded solemnly. "We all do. Fortunately, it's only the house at risk. They're safe and vacationing with the Morays."

Skiing. In the snow. I shivered again.

She moved back to the wheel. "Well, we better get going. Submerge for the storm and lock the tethers, and we'll see you another day."

Terra jumped up from where she'd listened to our conversation. "Mommy, can I give the mermaid a flower?"

Eartha agreed, but the boat was already drifting from the dock. Terra held out a white daisy which I couldn't reach. Afraid she might tumble overboard, I slid off my raft into the cool water and swam her way. A few strokes brought me to the side of the boat and I heaved myself up enough that she could tuck the flower behind my ear.

"Thank you for the flower, sweetie."

Terra ducked her head low and whispered in my ear. "Be nice to the sharks, pretty mermaid. They're not mean. They're misunderstood."

Before I could question her cryptic message, the boat puttered away, Eartha and Terra waving their good-byes.

I watched the boat disappear over the horizon. I switched my strokes and rolled onto my back, my breasts lolling to the sides to add their stabilizing effect, although their half-cup size difference wobbled me for a moment. My hair drifted out, its ends tickling my shoulders and back like silky strands of kelp and curious fish. The fluid rise and fall of the waves calmed me as nothing on land could. Meditation, ancient yoga, even my art… none of those brought me the peace and tranquility I'd known here on the lake.

Yes, water was definitely my Zen Garden.

The rumble in my belly finally enticed me out of the water. I hadn't eaten since morning, and I certainly hadn't spent any time on my painting. The siren call of the waves would have to wait. I hoisted myself from the water to dry off, then padded along the broad walkway encircling the house. Its all-glass structure glinted in the sun like a diamond, but the acres of sapphire blue waves were far more valuable to me.

In spite of their popular moniker, these *glass* houses were crafted from a transparent and pricey metal alloy. Only the wealthy could afford construction with such material and the privacy it required. Transparent walls wouldn't go over in the city where your neighbor's apartment was an arm's-length away. Here, I had a full-circle view of the lake, the house bathed in natural sunlight even on a cloudy day. After so many years crammed in the cities, staring out at the distant water and wondering why I was so unhappy, I realized it wasn't enough for me to *see* the water. I needed to *touch* it, to have it surround me and caress my skin like a lover. Too bad I wasn't the mermaid Terra called me. That would be heaven.

Once inside, I plucked an apple from the counter bowl and walked to the far wall where a fireplace burned with fake flames. It wasn't the reason I was drawn to that part of the house. My true fascination was the colored alloy embedded in the adjacent wall. Blues, aquas, grays, silvers, and a splash of gold. Tiny spots of color, like an ancient Earth pointillist painting, coalesced into an image that had kept me spellbound for hours during my weeks in the house. Up close, they were nothing but random dots, though lovely in their vibrancy and flow. But when my eyes focused on the image as a whole, the dots formed a merman. Perhaps the king of the sea. A warrior, judging by the gold spear he held in his strong grasp.

The artist's skill amazed. The colors had been expertly fused into the wall using a technique unfamiliar to me. Not paint, not glass, not a surface adhesive. The image must have been crafted when the wall itself had been manufactured. Yet, when I first saw and inquired about it, the Morays had shrugged off their ignorance. *It just showed up a few months ago* had been their explanation.

Apparently, the manufacturer denied having crafted it. The lake community office had no requisition for it. It just appeared overnight, as if someone had snuck in a house with only one door and an air lock seal to keep the outside... well, out; seamlessly merged his or her art into the wall in the course of a few hours when the alloy process took days; and did so with neither commission or request by the wealthy house owners nor a demand money or recognition.

None of it made sense, but how the image got there wasn't my concern. I could simply enjoy its presence. Taking up six feet of wall space was an artist's rendering of the sexiest man I'd ever seen, which was saying something because it was only half a man. Where the bare, muscular torso dipped into R-rated territory, a fish tail began. Long and powerful, like that of a large game fish. Swordfish or marlin. Dark blue and light gray with streaks of cerulean and silver along the sides, ending in a wide, crescent-shaped caudal fin.

More than just a naked chest and fish tail, the merman was handsome in a fierce, striking manner. Thick chunks of short navy hair waved in an unseen current. A long, straight nose with a slight point topped the knowing smirk on his lips. The gaze of his light gray eyes followed me around the room, tracking my movements like a hunter gleaning my strengths and weaknesses. Or the hot guy at the bar who was waiting for the first chance to buy me a drink and ask me to dance. Both possibilities kept me in an anticipatory state, my nerves heightened and my thoughts self-conscious. I'd seen the optical illusion before. I wasn't creeped out, but I wasn't about to go prancing around naked in front of it either.

His broad shoulders led to bulging biceps, and darned if my breath didn't catch each time I spied the capable fingers grasping the long, gold spear. I was accustomed to the slender hands of artists. These looked like the hands of physical labor. Strong. Rugged. Large enough to make even a curvy woman such as me feel dainty. Able to fight for the safety of his people and yet gentle enough to make one special woman quiver.

Oh, to be that woman.

If this image was meant to depict the king of the sea, he wasn't the stern man from ancient mythology, with flowing white hair and a beard. This depiction was a thirty-something with the strength and determination to command a planet's tides. He was the athletic team captain, the swoon-worthy rock star, the hunky guy next door, the brooding bad boy. Pretty much my every fantasy rolled into one man. He made my knees weak and my heart palpitate, and he wasn't even real.

"Bet you're breaking all kinds of mermaid hearts." I lifted

my half-eaten apple in salute and plopped on the couch. Maybe the weeks of solitude were getting to me if I was talking to the wall art. I loved the uncommon solitude here, but I was a naturally gregarious person. Friends joked that I'd talk to a wall if it would talk back. The fact my merman hadn't spoken a word apparently didn't dissuade me.

It might be silly, but his image had prompted all sorts of midnight fantasies. My legs wrapped around him while his large hands encompassed my breasts. My hands fisted his blue hair as my own locks encircled our entangled bodies. The familiar throb between my legs sprung to life.

I sighed in sexual frustration and glanced over at my current work-in-progress. I'd painted a perfect likeness of the merman... a copy of another artist's work. Given the circumstances, I wasn't overly guilty about this obvious plagiarism. I doubted a cat-burglar-turned-charitable-artist who sneaks into hermetically sealed houses to fuse his creations into the wall without the owners' knowledge or permission would hunt me down and sue me.

"I'll paint something original as soon as I finish." I made the promise as much to myself as to the merman and his anonymous creator. "I just need to get you out of my system."

Gah! Those words echoed what my last ex had said to me a few months ago. I hated them now as much as I had then. "I'm sorry, I didn't mean that. I meant that I'll start on something else as soon as I'm finished with you."

Ugh. That didn't sound much better. And why was I apologizing to an image on the wall?

Rather than stick my verbal foot in my mouth again, I jumped up and beelined for the kitchen, threw my apple core away, and plucked a bottle of white wine from the chiller. Glancing at the fancy label filled with words I didn't understand but assumed meant *if you have to ask you can't afford it*, I poured my dinner into a glass.

The setting sun washed the house in a golden red glow. The furniture looked bathed in blood. Dark clouds formed on the opposite horizon. An uneasy shiver raced down my spine. A sense of foreboding coursed through my veins. I'd never experienced harsh weather on the open water. I shouldn't worry, though. These houses were built to withstand cataclysmic forces, and the predicted storm didn't even register on the *holy shit* scale. The house and I would both be fine.

Still, I couldn't shake the sudden twinge in my nerves.

I turned mid-step and headed for the engine room. Within a few minutes, the huge structure was submerged and secured a safe distance from the water's surface. Normally, I would have been fascinated to watch the structure engulfed by water during the descent—is this what living under water would be like?—but my odd apprehension glued my eyes to the monitors rather than the rising water line outside. I pulled in a deep breath and slowly exhaled, hoping my nerves would calm. Nothing left to do but resume my evening.

I moseyed back to the couch.

The house was large enough to host a party of over a hundred guests comfortably, yet I was inexorably drawn to the cozy nook by the fireplace and the handsome merman. Maybe because I craved the companionship, such as it was. Part of me was an embarrassed schoolgirl caught gawking at the male nudes in the art museum. The other part was all woman, hoping for a peek at what might lie beneath the waist of his fishtail. Did the old adage about large hands hold true? Or, in the mer-world, did the size of his dorsal fin mean anything? And where did a merman hide his package? Inquiring—and apparently horny—minds wanted to know.

Setting my wine glass on the coffee table, I lounged against the couch cushions, staring at him. The house, now fully submerged deep in the waters, was made gloomier from the twilight and the approaching storm. Only the flickering ambient light from the fireplace illuminated him. Perhaps a result of the shadowy backdrop and dim light of the room, his eyes glowed with intensity. Angry. Violent. A warlord ready to battle his enemies, his eyes burning with purpose, his golden spear shimmering in the firelight.

I picked up a paintbrush. My own version of the merman was far less menacing. My gaze volleyed between the two images. Dare I proceed? I would only ruin what I'd begun without fully capturing the current mood of my subject.

Frustrated, I set my brush down and picked up my wineglass. I pulled a long sip into my mouth and pondered its nuances. Crisp and citrusy with a thin thread of sweetness. It reminded me of sushi, which made my belly rumble, the apple only having curbed my hunger briefly. Of course, my deeper hunger was of a more carnal nature, and had been left unsatisfied these past weeks. I swallowed the wine and it warmed a path to my stomach. A flush crept to my cheeks, although whether that heat was a result of the wine or the unblinking stare from the merman, I couldn't say. I licked my lips, my eyes never leaving his, and tilted the wine glass for another drink. "If I drink like a fish tonight, maybe you'll come to life and tongue-pound my salty oyster."

I winked at the merman for effect. Damn if it didn't appear like he winked back.

THUMP!

The loud boom woke me. The house shook from the reverberations and I tumbled off the couch and banged against the coffee table.

I had dozed off as the storm hit. This far below the surface, the storm was little more than an orange blip on the weather map. While the wind and waves raged up top, the house swayed gently on its moorings.

So why had I fallen off the couch?

THUMP!

The house rocked as if broadsided by something enormous. The structure shook from the impact and lurched to the side. I tumbled against the coffee table again, my brain too sleep-addled to stop my fall.

Holy mackerel! What could possibly wobble this mansion? Was I under attack by Opee Sea Killers? Battered by a school of giant Gooberfish?

THUMP!

I pulled to a stand as the house teetered. My heart thudded in my chest as loudly as the deep booms echoing in the room. I had no idea what the impact strength of the house's alloy was, but hoped the designers had taken into account possible siege by enormous and aggressive sea creatures never before discovered on Aquata Prime. My heart pounded, but my head was still hazy from wine and sleep. Or did sheer terror scatter my thoughts?

Out of habit, I looked at the merman, as if he might have answers. Stupid to expect wall art to save me, but perhaps I could find solace in the familiar. I didn't. Again, he seemed different. Changed. Urgency rippled through him, sending panic through my veins. His expression thunderous, like the weather so far above us. His spear glowed in the darkness. His free hand reached out to me, as if beckoning me into the safety of his arms. I placed my palms against the wall where his chest was. Cold, like the black water on the other side.

What was I expecting? Some cheesy made-for-TV movie damsel-in-distress rescue scene? I dropped my hands and shook my head to clear it. "This damsel's gonna go check the instruments. Hopefully there's an *in case of underwater attack* button."

I turned to head to the mechanical room—*THUMP!* The house heaved. I lost my footing and fell backward. Off balance, my arms flailed to the side. Maybe my merman would catch me before I hit.

Whack!

Dazed, I opened my eyes. The room was too dark to see. My head throbbed and my limbs moved as if in slow motion. My thoughts drifted and floated, caught by some weird current that ebbed and flowed yet remained elusive. Groggy. Languid.

This was the strangest hangover I'd ever experienced.

I shook my head and rubbed my eyes. I wasn't hungover. All I'd done last night was—*damn!*—I'd hit my head. Was this what a concussion felt like?

Or maybe the house had broken apart in the storm and now I was dead. That might explain the floating sensation. And the difficulty breathing. But not the odd tickle at my sides.

I looked around, trying to focus, but saw only blackness. Not even the fireplace was lit. The storm must have shorted out the power somehow. I'd have to feel my way to the mechanical room and hope my eyes would adjust to the darkness.

Something brushed my face each time I turned my head. Soft and silky. I flicked it away with my hand, but it returned almost immediately. The same brush of something soft against my shoulders and spine. I reared back, desperate to escape it, whatever it was, but it followed me, covering my face and hands.

Omigawd, I'm being attacked by fringe! My heart beat a staccato rhythm against my ribs. Adrenalin shot through my system and I gasped for air. I didn't remember this particular fabric accent in the house, and certainly not these long strands. What kind of hell was this?

"Calm down. You're safe here."

The man's deep voice only spurred my panic. Why was there a man in the house? How had he entered a sealed and submerged structure? *And why was this damn fringe still in my face?*

Firm hands clasped my arms and my palms grazed a muscular chest. *Holy mackerel!* A shirtless man was in the house! The fact should have heightened my hysteria, but the warmth which radiated up my arms—the strong, steady beat of his heart beneath my fingertips—somehow calmed my panic. The fringe swept away from my face. A soft glowing source of light to the side illuminated two beautiful gray eyes.

Two *familiar*, beautiful gray eyes.

I flinched away from the face of my merman. That fall must have bashed my head harder than I'd thought, and this was some crazy-real concussion-related hallucination. My gaze darted over the three-dimensional details of his face and the muscular, chiseled features of his torso that had invaded my dreams. A half-smile curled his lips as if he understood my mute confusion. A quick glance down proved he was indeed my merman. The thick fish body began where his Adonis muscles ended. As mouthwatering as the artist's rendering on the wall had been, it was nothing compared to flesh and blood.

My nipples pearled and warmth spread through my belly. If I was dreaming, I didn't want to wake up.

I must have stared at that spot a few pounding heartbeats too long. My merman chuckled. "They won't magically turn into legs. Believe me, I've tried."

My gaze shot back up to his. I gasped, but didn't hear the rush of air from my mouth. When I spoke, my voice was strangely gargled. "Why would you want your beautiful tail to become legs?"

Releasing one of my arms, he scrubbed a hand through his short strands of navy hair—I might have moaned at the striking view of his bicep muscles—then turned to pluck his glowing gold spear from where it rested against the wall. I definitely moaned then, catching the view of my merman's firm backside. The flat image on the wall hadn't allowed for this full effect and… well, it was a work of art.

He turned back to me, one eyebrow raised as if he couldn't guess what I'd moaned about, and brought the spear to rest at his side. It was the room's only source of light, its glow casting an intimate circle around us, barely illuminating a stone bench in the center of the room and a curtain of sorts to the side. The fact we were alone in the otherwise bare room added to the sense of intimacy. His other hand slid to mine and he lifted my knuckles to press his full lips against them. My breath hitched when he leaned over as if in a small bow.

"You'll have a thousand questions, and I'll gladly answer them all as best I can. But first, introductions." He swung his spear as if to encompass the entire room and everything beyond it. "I'm Prince Eric. Welcome to Atlantia."

I stared at him, my mouth agape, and no doubt a look of utter disbelief mixed with growing horror on my face. He smiled, laughter dancing in his eyes. This was more than a wine-addled dream, and I shook my head to dislodge the influence of whatever mind-altering substance I must have ingested.

"Prince? Atlantia? I'm sorry, but that's a myth, and this joke isn't funny. I think I need medical attention. I'm sure I have a concussion and there are long filaments in my vision." I blinked hard, hoping to dislodge them.

He laughed. I was about to yell at him for being heartless, but he swept his hand to the side and my vision cleared.

"This is no joke." His tone still carried a bubble of good humor. He didn't sound at all repentant. Rather than anger me, his deep rumbling tenor calmed and aroused. The beauty of his voice was another aspect I hadn't been able to appreciate while staring at his mural. "Yes, I am the Prince of Atlantia. No, you don't have a concussion. Those aren't filaments in your vision, it's your hair. And might I say, you make a stunning mermaid."

Uh... mermaid?

In spite of his claim, this was surely some kind of joke. Had Eartha set this up? I remembered Terra's insistence on calling me a pretty mermaid. Perhaps this was some lake community initiation to mess with the newbie's mind. So not funny of them to tease me with the temptation of being a mermaid. More cruel than dangling a strip of bacon in front of a carnivore.

I jerked my hand from his and wagged my finger at him, dragging in a deep breath to give him all kinds of hell. Then he dropped his spear low, letting its glow illuminate my bare legs.

What the fu—

They weren't legs.

Below the hem of my *Painters do it with Broad Strokes* shirt, where there should have been two long and pale legs, was a sheath of emerald green covered in iridescent scales, ending with a long, flowing fin. Not sure how or when he and Eartha had sheathed my legs in this casing. Normally, I'd be thrilled to wear a mermaid-skirt and pretend it was real for a while, but this practical joke had already worn thin.

I wiggled my legs inside the skin-tight material. Nothing happened. Not just that my legs didn't move, but I couldn't feel them. Couldn't sense them as separate limbs with inner and outer thighs, kneecaps, and ankles. I tried to wiggle my toes and the soft rays of my lush *va-va-voom* tail fin fanned and flicked.

I reached under my shirt's hem to push the skirt material off. Finding the seam where my hips met the sleek, almost rubbery texture, I dug a fingernail in to pull the material away. It didn't budge and I only managed to gouge myself. Wincing, I tried a difference spot, with the same result. If they'd glued it to my skin, it was a damn good job. No seam, no fabric edge I could pick at, and I felt the brush of my fingers as readily against the skirt as I did my side. As if it was a natural continuation of my skin, like how my sensitive lips transition to my sensitive-in-a-totally-different-way cheeks.

My gut clenched. It couldn't be true, but my heart sang with hope that it was. I could barely whisper, afraid that speaking it would wake me from a crazy-realistic dream. If I woke up, I'd miss the chance to enjoy this. "I'm a mermaid?"

A large hand grasped mine again. I looked up at him. A thousand questions screamed in my head, but not a peep came forth.

He nodded as if he knew exactly what I was going through. "Yes, you're a mermaid. You fell through a magic portal and transformed into a creature of the sea. Please don't ask how. I know I said I'd answer all your questions, but that one is beyond my pay grade."

His claim defied logic, and I should be freaking out. But I was an artist, a creative sort of person who rarely let logic override my love of what could be. Or at least my reservoir of possibilities. And if what he was saying—and what my eyes were seeing—was true, my fondest dream had just come true. "I'm a mermaid?"

He nodded again, the well of his patience much deeper than my comprehension at the moment. What was wrong with me? Why did I continue to question this? Was I hoping for a different answer? I'd dreamed of being a mermaid my entire life. Even if this was a dream, why was I wasting time fighting it and not enjoying myself? I'd worked hard to end up at a lake house, surrounded by water. I should *carpe* the hell out of this mermaid *diem*.

He squeezed my hand to get my attention and smiled, like he knew the thought process that had whipped through my mind and exactly when I had arrived at the point to give this adventure a whirl. His thumb rubbed over my knuckles, sending shivers down my spine straight to my core. "We should have a swimming lesson."

I snorted. I didn't want swim lessons. I wanted adventure, singing fish, and spontaneous dance scenes. "I'm a perfectly capable swimmer."

He flashed me a smile that would have made my knees go weak. If I had knees.

"With legs, perhaps. But this takes a different skill-set. Trust me." He pulled me forward. I tried to kick, to undulate in an amateurish butterfly stroke. I only succeeded in convulsing and rolling to the side. His hand on my waist stopped my efforts. I gulped at how his warm hands practically spanned my width. "You don't have hip or knee joints anymore. Our lower skeleton is strongest in a side-to-side motion. Pretend you're parading through a crowded bar trying to catch someone's eye."

"You want me to walk through a bar? With no legs?"

"Yeah. You know. Strut your stuff. Swing your hips." He leaned close enough to whisper in my ear. "Make every man want you."

The mental image of his words and the warmth of his breath against my neck washed another shiver of need over me. My nipples puckered, and I couldn't blame the room's ambient temperature this time. My merman—the one whose image had inspired all manner of fantasies these past weeks—was now within arms' reach, urging me to make him want me.

Hell yeah, I could do this.

After more awkward jerks from my unresponsive tail, I eased into a slow side-to-side wave originating from where my hips should have been. The motion used muscles in my torso I didn't realize existed. Would I finally carve out that narrow waistline I'd always wanted? Prince Eric kept pace beside me, his broad smile and nod of approval warmed me all along my lateral line. The instinctive flare of my fins was a strange sensation as I worked my way around the room.

"Great job. You're a natural." He released my hand and then backed toward the wall. "You ready to take that tail out for a spin?"

I stared at him, hesitant. His hair streamed in short waves atop his head, and his bold tail moved slightly to keep him suspended in the middle of the room. His lips curled in the achingly familiar come-hither smirk that was both invitation and challenge. The handsome merman proffered his hand in the same way his image on the Morays' wall had last night.

Did I dare take him up on it? What would happen if I did?

What would happen if I didn't?

Whatever magic or dream had turned me into a mermaid, I wouldn't find answers or adventures waiting in this dark room. I'd have to venture forth. And maybe entice a kiss from the prince's full lips. Would it be as wonderful as I'd imagined? Why was that the first thing to come to mind? And how could I make it happen?

I slanted him my most flirtatious smile. "So do I call you Prince Eric or Your Majesty?"

He laughed, shaking his head as if embarrassed. "Actually, we're pretty casual around here. Just call me Eric."

I held my hand out for him to shake. "I'm Ariel LaRue. Pleased to meet you."

He gripped my hand and tugged, the slight pull drifting my body straight into his until my breasts pressed against his chest. My lungs heaved in anticipation. My lips quivered and I drug in a deep breath of…

Wait. Was I really breathing water?

"Eric, this whole mermaid thing is wild. How is it that I'm breathing water and not drowning?" Funny how breathless my voice sounded when I didn't have any air in my lungs.

"Gills." He lifted his arm over his head and nodded to his side. "They come with the tail."

Grateful for the reason to stare at his chest, I looked closer. Sure enough, along the angle of his obliques were several slashes in his skin. With each exhale, they opened, and I spied pink frills within. Trying to be gentle, I ran my fingers along the seam. Eric hissed and clasped my hand against his side.

I jerked back on a yelp. "I'm sorry! I didn't mean to hurt you."

"You didn't." His laugh was strangled. "They're just... ticklish. You have your own, if you want to, uh, check them out."

Tickle my own gills? Wait, I had gills? I hadn't seen my obliques since I was twelve and developed a chest with its own gravitational pull. I laughed and waved the hem of my shirt. "Not sure that's possible, Eric."

But you *can fondle my gills.* The offer caught in my throat. He might make my nether regions moist, but I knew nothing about this merman. Prince or not, that didn't mean he was everything I'd imagined him to be while staring at his image on the wa—

Wait a sec. "Eric, do you sneak into glass houses and adhere your likeness to the walls?" With a wave of my hand, I cleared the floating strands of hair away from my face.

Eric pulled his gaze up from my breasts with visible effort, shrugging at being caught ogling me. He shook his head. "This is Atlantia, not Aquata Prime. All water, no houses. Besides, I'm a community manager, not an artist."

He cleared his throat. "On a different topic, I like your... shirt. But if you want, I can schedule a shell-fitting for you."

My eyes surely bugged out. "You have shells this big?"

He laughed, a chuckle that vibrated deliciously along the hairs on my skin, and grabbed my hand, pulling me through a doorway I hadn't noticed before. I swam beside him down the large hall, concentrating on my newfound skills.

"Actually, many mermaids choose not to cover themselves at all." He resumed the conversation as we traveled. "They prefer to go natural. You're more than welcome to do so as well. The effects of gravity are less prominent here."

The low dip of his voice at the end made it obvious he hoped I might accept that offer, and enticed me to do just that.

That was for sure. Where my breasts usually tugged at my chest and pulled on my back, their mass was now negligible. I glanced down, thrilled at how perky they were and surprised their buoyancy hadn't shot me straight to the surface. I'd always been drawn to water, and having natural life preservers was one of the many reasons why. Water freed my body from the detractors of its own shape and size. While I'd never be streamlined by any definition, I loved how easily I moved through water, its texture a soft caress against my skin and even scales. Water supported me, embraced me, lifted me... Except for the fact it couldn't provide me with mind-blowing sex, water was everything I wanted in a boyfriend.

I released Eric's hand and twirled awkwardly. My breasts swayed and bobbed as if the currents of water were faithful lovers. My nipples were tight buds of arousal. I crossed my arms over them and shimmied back to Eric, hoping he didn't realize how turned on I was.

"A, uh, shell-fitting would probably be wise." My cheeks heated.

He nodded, his knowing gaze flicking to my chest before meeting my eyes. The slow smile that spread across his lips made it obvious he hadn't missed a thing, but chose not to comment. I shrugged and tossed my hair from my face. "The water's cold."

His laugh followed as we continued forward. The hall transitioned from dark and barren to light and amazing as it opened into an enormous cavern carved out of a coral reef. The walls were pocked with waving anemones in a kaleidoscope of colors, their papillae like a stubbly carpet dancing in the current. Opalescent spires carved with swarms of exotic sea creatures twisted from the floor to the ceiling several stories above. From there hung delicate pearls strung in glowing chandeliers that cast warm, dancing light on everything.

"Is this the Atlantian palace?" I ogled the opulent room, certain my mouth hung agape.

"Yes. This is technically the throne room. The central hub and marketplace of the palace. All Atlantian citizens are welcome here." Eric motioned to where a gilded path wound its way along the rocky floor and ascended to the middle of a far wall. A wide dais held a giant scallop shell throne adorned with winking jewels. The throne sat empty.

"Central hub and marketplace?" I glanced around. Hundreds of hallways opened into the cavernous space. Merfolk, fish, and other aquatic lifeforms I'd never before seen or imagined passed through the hall, making it a major thoroughfare not unlike the streets of the cities on Aquata Prime. Booths and stacks of items littered the floor of the room, the noise of commerce and bartering a constant din in the water.

By contrast, the throne and dais were vacant.

"Where does the king hold court?"

"There is no king. There is only me, and I'm not a throne kind of guy."

I turned to him. "No king? Did he die? I'm sorry for your loss."

Eric pulled upright and released my hand to run his fingers through thick waves of navy hair. I struggled not to gawk at the flex of his bicep. His voice was rough with tension. "Ariel, the Atlantian king unfortunately died years ago. But I'm not his son. I'm just a community manager and I never knew the king. You don't have to express any condolences to me for that loss."

He'd mentioned his occupation before, but I hadn't grasped its significance. I crossed my arms under my breasts. "What do you mean, *community manager?* You're a prince, right?"

He shrugged. "The Atlantians call me Prince, I think mostly because they don't know what else to call me. Their king died in a battle against the Sharkanians. He didn't have any offspring or successor, and I have experience coordinating projects and personnel. I stepped up to help in their time of need, and they decided I was the most qualified to run the place."

His gaze landed on my chest again. "Besides, I have decidedly un-princely thoughts with you around."

When he spoke like that, his tone vibrating through my bones like a battery-operated toy, all of my questions flicked away more swiftly than a school of herring faced with a hungry tuna. Speaking of hungry, my mouth watered for a taste of my merman.

Before I could ask him to spout details of his thoughts, Eric clasped my hand again and ushered me into the open area of the great hall. The passing merfolk nodded respectfully to him and stared at me with something akin to shocked wonder. Excited whispers of "that's the one" and "she's here" rang through the great hall. Those who didn't turn to stare at us were busy wrestling with another, or dancing, or engaged in some sort of full body contact—

Wait. What the...

"Eric, are those merpeople having sex?" I tried to whisper discreetly, but surprise might have affected my volume. Fortunately, no one seemed to notice my outburst.

His shoulders shook from the effort not to laugh. "Um, yeah. You'll find that Atlantians and other sea creatures aren't overly modest about their procreation practices. In fact, they pretty much just do it wherever and whenever. Survival of the horniest, I guess."

I tried to laugh at his joke, but was too overwhelmed by the sheer pluck of the fucking couples. Would he expect me to copulate with him in the middle of the throne room market? Would he even want to copulate with me? I might not want to have sex for all to witness, but the thought of making love to Eric was an intriguing concept. Hell, who was I kidding? I wanted him to want me as much as I wanted him.

Before I could broach the subject, a small group of dull gray merfolk approached us. Their faces were flatter, broader, their mouths tight-lipped gashes and their noses mere holes between their wide-set eyes. Even though they had the requisite body parts above their fish tails, they were way more fish-like all over than Eric or myself. Each member of the group wore a decorative mantle of woven kelp and colorful shells, where the other merpeople I'd spotted wore nothing. These must be dignitaries, government officials, or other important individuals. Before I could ask, the first three bowed low to Eric, their arms sweeping wide. Skin extended between their spiny fingers, no doubt to help propel them through water.

The front merman rose, signaling the others to follow, and addressed Eric in dulcet tones of reverence. "Prince Eric, we are honored you have brought us another like you. Her coloring is the vibrant beauty of the reef itself."

"Ambassador, may I introduce you to Lady Ariel. She comes to us from my home world of Aquata Prime. I hope you will welcome her as easily as you did me." Eric spoke in poised, regal tones. No wonder they called him a prince. Here was a man who could ease doubts and instill confidence with just a few words. Everything about him screamed *capable,* and although I'm sure that served him well as both a community manager and prince, I only cared how that translated into his bedroom skills.

After months without sex, three weeks staring at the image of a total hottie, and a few minutes in his presence—and a mer-orgy all around me—I was primed to learn just how far I could take this mermaid fantasy. Thankfully, Eric had the presence of mind to urge me forward by the hand he still held. Face to face with the Ambassador cooled my desire. Maybe he was considered attractive to other Atlantians, but he didn't hold a glowstick to my merman.

"A pleasure to meet you, Ambassador." I dipped into an awkward curtsy and extended my hand for a shake.

The Ambassador grasped my hand between both of his, holding it like it was a treasured bauble. His skin was surprisingly warm against mine, even as his scaly hands were rough as fine-grade sand paper. His mouth widened in what I assumed was a smile and his round eyes slanted upward. "May the waters always be warm and the currents always at your back, Lady Ariel. You bless us to arrive and fulfill the prophe—"

"Ambassador, I'm sure you have other duties to attend to." Eric cut him off. "I will make sure you have more opportunity to speak with Lady Ariel. But for now, she is learning about our home."

"Of course. My apologies." The Ambassador released my hand and bowed to Eric. "We cannot speed the waves. They rise and fall as Our Mother wills them, and any interference from us is only so much careless splashing."

On those cryptic words, which held the tone of philosophy or doctrine, the Ambassador and his entourage swam away. I turned toward Eric, baffled by the exchange. As if he could read my mind, he shrugged. "The Ambassador is more like a religious leader here. They have some sayings they spout that will seem weird now, but you get used to them."

Like meeting new people on Aquata Prime, some took a longer adjustment period. And since I doubted I'd be here long enough to worry about the Ambassador's strange remarks and why Eric cut him off mid-sentence, I just shrugged.

With a warm hand spanning my lower back, he urged me forward. As we continued through the grand hall, I noticed more merpeople whispering and pointing.

"Eric, why is everyone, I mean the ones not having sex, staring at me and whispering?"

He took a few moments to answer. "Ariel, your beauty is stunning. It's only natural some merfolk might stare."

He spoke the compliment like claiming water was wet. Yes, I'd been told countless times I was beautiful. I had a string of exes proving that flattery was just a means to an end. What sort of end was Eric hoping for? The tingles radiating up my spine from where his fingers lightly traced my skin hoped his wants aligned with mine. Like, in terms of a horizontal alignment. Damn if his touch wasn't messing with the focus of my thoughts. I tugged them back to our conversation.

"Beauty is only scale-deep, Eric." Did he hear the cynicism in my voice?

He pulled me up against his chest, forcing my attention on him. With a few swings of his strong tail, he carried us into a small hallway, away from the crowd and looks and whispers. Another thrust of his tail, and he backed me against the wall, its cool stone surface a sharp contrast to his smooth skin and body heat. He caressed my cheek with the back of his hand, his eyes roving over my face is if memorizing it.

"Ariel, beauty is found everywhere. You just have to know how to look for it." He added his other hand and cupped my face, a thumb rubbing my bottom lip. I wanted desperately to pull the digit into my mouth and nibble on its thick pad. I wanted him to kiss me like I was the oxygen his body needed. Instead, he blinked himself out of whatever daze and pressed his hands against the wall behind me, trapping me within his arms without touching me further. Regret pulled his expression. "Your beauty is so much more than how much your body beckons to mine. More than how much pleasure we could find in each other's arms. It's the sparkle of humor in your eyes. The natural rise of your lips, like they prefer a smile to a frown. The kindness in your voice."

He pulled back, drifting so I no longer felt his body heat. "I'm no expert, but I've known enough women to understand the difference between someone I just want to fuck and someone I'd like to get to know."

His expression defied me to prove him wrong, but my heart had turned to goo. I pushed off the wall and drifted past him, keeping my gaze locked with his as I turned. "I'll assume you consider me the latter. Treat me right, and I could be the former as well."

Eric snort-coughed and muttered something that sounded like *you already are.* Before I could question it, he led me down the hallway, away from the throne room. The act of swimming took all of my concentration, so our conversation lagged. He let me set the slow, arduous pace through the halls, showering me with encouragement and compliments at my progress. "The learning curve might be a bit steep, but you're getting the hang of it."

"You know this for certain?"

"Absolutely. Like you, I'm not a natural-born mer-person, in case that fact wasn't already obvious. I was a lake community manager on Aquata Prime. Several years ago, I was checking on a code issue at one of the houses. A storm hit and the waves knocked me into the wall. I fell through the magic portal and woke up here looking like this." He nodded to indicate his fish body.

His story bounced around my head, touching on my recent conversation with Eartha. "Lake community manager? I'm housesitting at Lake Triton, and their manager is missing, too. Sounds like a conspiracy. What's going on?"

"He's not *missing, too.* He's me. But I'm surprised they haven't filled that job in all this time."

"*All this time?* You've only been missing for a few months. Not years."

He stared at me, blinking as if to process my news. Then he cleared his throat and shrugged. "I guess time is different here. Believe me, it's been years."

If time did move differently here, then I needed to stay vigilant of its passage. Otherwise, I might get so caught up in this amazing adventure that the Morays could return from vacation and wonder what the hell happened to their house sitter. I'd never get another house-sitting job if I wasn't there when they returned. Instead, I'd be stuck in the city for the rest of my life, choking on the claustrophobic proximity of everything. This was all assuming the house had even survived the storm or whatever had caused me to stumble and bash my head. All that strain to the house's structure couldn't possibly be good for it.

My gut clenched as the weight of responsibility slammed down. What if the house had been damaged? What if it was sinking to the bottom of Lake Triton at this moment? I had to return to Aquata Prime immediately.

"Eric, this has been fun and interesting and a dream come true, and I've really enjoyed talking with you, but I gotta get back." Which meant I'd have to leave him, and the thought was a like poking a hole in a floatation device. My heart blew a sad raspberry as it deflated.

"Get back where?"

"Home. Well, I mean the lake house I'm sitting for while the owners are on vacation. There was a huge storm and it might be damaged, and I need to be there when they return."

Eric began shaking his head before I'd even finished. "There's no going back, Ariel. I'm sorry, but this is your new home."

My dream turned to a nightmare. "What do you mean *there's no going back*? Can't I just find the magic portal and return to Aquata Prime?"

Again, he shook his head while I still spoke. "Believe me, if it were that easy, I wouldn't have been missing all these years. Er, months. The portal is a one-way street."

My stomach was a Lake Triton-sized boulder in my gut. "Maybe it moves? Maybe the one-way street back to home is somewhere else. Have you looked for it? Surely it's somewhere out there."

He turned away. His fists clenched and he took a deep breathe before releasing it. He struggled with some internal battle, and when he turned back to me, his eyes were filled with anger, hurt, and desperation. His voice was barely a whisper. "Atlantia has no rumor or myth about a place where merfolk go and never return. Aquata Prime's merfolk myths are eons old, probably dating back to ancient Earth. If there was a return portal, don't you think someone here would have stumbled upon it within the last few centuries? Don't you think there would be merfolk sightings on Aquata Prime and grainy pictures handed up as proof and mermaid hunters on the prowl around the globe?"

I couldn't accept his words. Their truth meant my fate was sealed. As much as I liked the idea of being a mermaid, I had assumed it would be temporary. The fact it might be permanent was a tough bite to swallow. I spoke around the hard lump in my throat. "Aquata Prime has a lot of water to hide in."

He ran his fingers through his hair, and this time I could almost ignore his biceps. "Merfolk wouldn't keep hidden in the depths of Aquata Prime. They're fascinated with my tales of cities above the ocean surface and creatures that can't breathe water. Air-breathing people who choose to live surrounded by an element that could kill them is the stuff of scary campfire stories here, if we could have campfires. Which means no one from here has gone there. Believe me."

"Believe you? That's all?" My voice climbed with hysteria. "You haven't heard any empirical evidence that there might be a return portal, and you're satisfied with that? *Well, no one's ever heard of it, so I guess I'm just stuck here?*"

Rage flared in his eyes as I mocked him in a nasally voice. I didn't care because he didn't seem to care. The luster on the grand adventure of being a mermaid dulled significantly when that adventure became a life sentence. The thought of eating nothing but ice cream for an entire day also seemed fun, but I wouldn't want to have to do it forever.

His body tense as if battling against itself for control. His face a mask of pain. He fairly vibrated with emotion, the intensity rippling off him in waves that threatened to knock me over. "What do you want me to say, Ariel?" He growled, but I heard the loss, the anguish, the... utter hopelessness, in that rumble. "I've searched all of Atlantia for a portal back home. I miss my family and friends so much I can barely breathe. I hope my mom's forgotten me rather than worrying about what happened to her son who disappeared without a trace. Every single day I wake up, I have to force myself *not* to swim into a hydrothermal vent and end it all."

He raked his hands through his hair, then scrubbed his mouth with the palm. "I'm sorry."

My tears blended with the surrounding water. I shook my head and tried to speak, but anguish held me in its crushing embrace and I gulped in breaths between sobs. Unable to watch the rawness of his pain, I covered my eyes and let my hair drift around me while I cried. For my loss, yes, but mostly for his.

Warm arms surrounded me and pulled me against his broad, powerful chest. His hands circled my back in calming strokes. "I'm so sorry, Ariel." His murmur against my temple was a balm to my tumultuous emotions. Emotions not even half as tormented as his. I was surrounded by the strength and comfort of someone who had been in my fins and survived. Someone who had carved a path for himself. Someone who could help me find my own way, if this was where my fate had brought me.

My artistic soul—ever the adventurous optimist—slithered up through all my grief and reminded me of my childhood longing to leave the noisy cities of Aquata Prime. My love of water. My I'd-trade-legs-for-fins-in-a-heartbeat dreams of being a mermaid. Maybe, just maybe, this was exactly where I was meant to be and everything before this had been merely waiting for my real life to begin. Then my heart pointed out the fact I was in the arms of a handsome man who had just set aside his own years of suffering to give me comfort for mine. And when had any of my exes ever been that thoughtful and selfless?

I took a deep breath and exhaled my anguish through my gills. Then I murmured against his chest. "Don't be sorry. I shouldn't have lashed out at you. This isn't your fault."

He traced a fingertip down my arm, then clasped my hand, squeezing gently as if that little move could make it all better. I clung to his warmth. He eased away and flicked his tail to resume our journey. The wink he slanted at me was all come-hither, his earlier desolation gone or buried deep.

Nodding his head in the direction we swam, he smiled. "Come on, I think our destination may go a long way in helping."

Another adventure? Definitely a challenge I couldn't help but accept, letting my earlier distress slough away like dirt in a shower. We emerged from the tunnel to an endless ocean. The throne room was vibrant with color and opulence, but before me were rolling, twisting hills of coral spread out as far as the eye could see until they disappeared into the murky distance. Colorful creatures—yes, some having sex—carpeted the coral, towering clusters of kelp dotted the landscape, and a myriad of aquatic lifeforms crawled, swum, undulated, zipped, fucked, and coiled among the dense jungle of anemone and sea urchins. Sure, the view lacked the pearly chandeliers of the throne room, but made up for that with its spectacular dance of life. My artist's eye soaked it up, snapshotting it in my memories.

Unlike the extremes of Aquata Prime's population density, Atlantia was simultaneously crowded and spacious. As we made our way through the throngs of creatures—some familiar in color and form, some unlike anything I could imagine...and I had a vivid imagination—I had plenty of room to move. Even surrounded by what should be a crush of bodies, there was nothing claustrophobic or constricting. Rather than feeling inhibited by proximity, joy and energy coursed through me.

"This is amazing, Eric. I wish I was a poet so I could find the words to express just how beautiful all this is."

When he didn't respond, I pulled my focus from the swirling beauty surrounding me to look at him. My heart lurched. He stared at me with an intensity I felt to the tips of my fin like an electric current. Like when the gray eyes of his likeness on the wall had tracked my every move, the power of his gaze now left me bare, exposed. I couldn't decipher the thoughts going through his mind, but felt their weight. I ventured a whisper to pull him back to the present. "Eric?"

"When I first arrived here, I also wished to be a poet with the words to describe what I saw." His lips twitched upward, but the power of his gaze did not ease. "I'd never seen anything so worthy of ballads and sonnets. Until I laid eyes on you."

My heart stopped, and when it beat again, it beat only for Eric. A lot of people had called me beautiful over the years, but those declarations never held such raw vulnerability. As if the stars glittered and planets rotated by my every wish. How could I not melt even more for him?

Eric cleared his throat, breaking the tender moment where he'd laid bare his soul and I'd stood there struck dumb and mute by his admission. "Ariel, when I apologized earlier, it wasn't for making you cry, although I feel bad for that as well. I meant I'm sorry you're in the same boat as me now. Away from home. Alone. No hope of going back."

I'd been on my own for years without family, having carved out a life wherever I landed. Eric seemed to have strong ties which had been snapped when he'd fallen through the portal to Atlantia. As great as my loss might be, his was worse. My heart broke again for him.

I shrugged, even though the attempt at nonchalance took effort. The reality of my predicament still weighed heavily. I could make the best of the situation, with his help. "Maybe I'm still in denial, but the difference is that I have you to guide me, right? I hate that you were alone for so long."

Eric flashed me a brief smile. "I was fortunate enough to find my niche. It keeps me busy and gives me purpose. We'll do the same for you."

"Not sure that's possible." My gut dropped as the truth hit home. "You see, I'm an artist."

"Yes, I gathered you're a painter from your shirt. Why is that an issue?"

I stopped and faced him. Had I really fallen into a wonderful watery world where my fantasy merman lived as king and I was a sexy mermaid, only to have the irony of my situation be a cruel punchline? "My medium is watercolors."

Shock, then amusement lit his face. He seemed to fight it, but the laughter burst forth. Normally, I might be pissed, but the throaty sound of his humor spurred my own. At least my predicament was my joke to tell, and he needed the laugh more than anyone I knew.

Eric regained his composure. "I guarantee we will find an alternate medium for you here." He reached out and gently pushed a wisp of hair from my face, his warm finger tracing from temple to chin. "Sand castles, maybe. Seashell roses. Kelp tapestries."

I swatted his hand away, but couldn't keep from laughing at the ridiculous suggestions. Two large hands framed my face and the laughter died in my throat, replaced by a lump I couldn't explain.

"Ariel, please don't be discouraged. Trust me when I say you truly belong here with us among the waters."

He dipped his head and brushed a chaste kiss across my lips. Sparks traveled from where our lips touched to each nerve ending and capillary in my body. I opened my mouth, hungry for more as he deepened the kiss. Warmth spread through me and a whirlpool caught my brain in its undertow. I clutched Eric's shoulders, hanging on for dear life, afraid something would rip me away from the magic of his kisses. His strong arms banded around my waist, anchoring me to his body and to the electric point where our lips met.

It was a kiss beyond any of my dreams. And I'd had some pretty wild ones after staring at Eric's image on the Morays' wall. Still, my fantasies were nothing compared to the real thing. Heat and need built, eager to take this kiss to the next level.

When we came up for air, I panted, gulping in the cool water.

Eric rested his forehead against mine, his breaths quick, needy bursts. "Who needs a hydrothermal vent? Your kisses set me on fire."

Voices in the distance pulled us both from the haze of sexual desire. Angry voices raised in confrontation. Eric's good humor vanished and he took my hand, leading me over to a secluded cluster of rocks. "As much as I'd like to continue what we started, I'm afraid I have a dispute to mediate."

"Can I watch you in action?"

He coughed. "Probably best if you stay here until you get yourself under control a bit." He nodded toward my tail, then leaned closer. "By the way, I love how the carpet matches the curtains."

I looked to where he motioned. There, in the middle of my fin—where the apex of my thighs would meet if I were still human—blossomed a small anemone with frilly pink fronds like so much antique lace.

"How did that get there?" I tried to brush it off, but shards of pleasure shattered through my body and I froze, biting back the moan which burst forth. I stared at Eric with what was surely disbelief. "What just happened? Is that my—?"

Eric nodded. "Yes, it is. The exact physiology is different, but the concept is the same. We don't get to hide our arousal anymore."

I looked down at his fishtail, which remained unchanged. "I guess I'm not a very good kisser."

Yes, I sounded petulant. No, I didn't care.

Eric cupped my cheek. "I've had a few years to wrangle my sea snake into submission, so to speak. Believe me, when I first discovered it, I was like a teenage boy again. Fortunately, mer-reproduction doesn't work with random floating sperm, or I'd have an army of offspring."

He swung an arm to indicate the vast waters. His meaning hit me, and I pulled back. "You mean every breath I take, I could be inhaling your sperm?"

He lifted a shoulder. "Not only mine. And not only sperm. Think about it."

"Ew! You mean I'm also breathing fish piss?" I covered my mouth as if it was an effective filter. My stomach roiled. "Holy mackerel, this puts a whole new spin on swallowing versus spitting."

He choked on his laugh. "What do you think you breathed in from the air back on Aquata Prime? The concept is the same, and just as unavoidable. Best not to overthink some things. But on the bright side, we have as much fresh fish and crab and caviar as you can eat. As a mermaid, you don't ever have to shave your legs again. Or wash your hair. Or worry that your makeup will run when you cry."

"Or worry I taste like fish, because everything does?"

He licked his lips, looking intrigued by my accidental suggestion. I hadn't meant to put thoughts of oral sex in his head. If the barest brush of my own fingertips caused so much pleasure, the thought of what his soft tongue could do nearly sent me into orgasmic convulsions.

I pushed him toward the ever-rising sounds of disagreement. "Tell you what. You go do your thing while I explore myself. When you're finished, assuming I'm also finished, you can show me more of my new home."

Eric sucked in a breath. His hands clasped my waist and he

growled. "You keep those silky fronds nice and warm and I'll be back soon enough to prove to you it's better down where it's wetter."

He claimed another deep kiss, then let go and swam toward the angry voices.

I rested against the rocky slope and let my mind wander for a moment. Mere hours before, I'd been a two-legged human fantasizing about the image of a handsome merman. Now, I was a mermaid in my own right with that same handsome merman promising sexual satisfaction. Maybe I'd hit my head and all this was a concussion-prompted dream. If it was, I wasn't about to turn prudish now. And if it wasn't, he was still the sexiest man to ever promise me a good time.

I closed my eyes, half-listening to the now-calm discussion going on over the ridge. With languid strokes, I wafted water over my engorged frills. Each wave caused tingles to skitter out to my extremities. Not enough to take me to the crest of my climax, but enough to keep me aroused. If I kept it up, I was going to blow the moment Eric touched me, but I couldn't quite stop. It simply felt too good.

"Such a beautiful creature should not be left alone."

Good feeling gone. The stranger's voice shattered my mood like an ice bath. I pulled up straight, my arousal retracting. A merman floated in front of me, muscled and fierce like a warrior. Brilliant, metallic blue except for the strip of white descending from his chest to the sharp angles of his tail. His large, lidless eyes were entirely black, yet expressive and filled with intelligence. He stared at me like a hunter sizing up his prey. Or a sexual rake sizing up his next conquest. A roguish smile curled his lips upward, revealing dual rows of sharp teeth made to rend flesh from bone. My blood turned to ice and a tremor of fear shot up my spine.

Shark.

I swallowed my panic. He might have the features of a mindless killer, but he also had the look of someone who could be reasoned with. Something in the way he pulled his lips down to hide his teeth when I gasped. In the slight furrow of his brow, as if he hoped—against doubt—I'd welcome him. It stilled my fin, keeping me rooted there instead of racing toward Eric. Unsure if I should encourage the sharkman's friendship, I certainly didn't want to be hurtful. So I opted for noncommittal with a side of confident. "I was alone for a reason. But I'm not without an escort. He'll be back shortly."

"Your escort must be a fool to leave your side. The ocean can be a dangerous place. So many predators around."

I cocked my head to the side and crossed my arms over my chest. "And you're just a nice guy looking for a damsel to protect?"

His smile faded and his jaw muscle ticked. Suspicion had filled my voice, but he didn't seem mad I lumped him with those dangerous predators he'd mentioned. He seemed resigned. Disappointed even. His gaze drifted to a distant point to his left. "We don't hunt for food all of the time. Sometimes conversation is a nice change of pace."

Those words held every bit the sound of rote repetition that the Ambassador's had. How many times had this sharkman repeated them to disbelieving ears? How many creatures assumed his shark half meant he had nothing else to offer but teeth and an indiscriminate appetite? I couldn't stop the compassion that welled up inside. "Look, where I come from, even the most unsuspecting person can turn out to be dangerous. Anyone can be a threat. Which also means, by contrast, that anyone can be a friend."

His expression had closed off, but now a look of reserved hope lit his eyes. I wasn't about to go for a swim alone with him, but my intuition told me I wasn't going to end up on his dinner menu, either. He smiled, a shy uptick of his lips without exposing his deadly teeth. "Allow me to protect you from harm."

A bright streak of gold speared the water between us. The sharkman jerked backward.

"Your normal manner of attack is more direct, Mako." Eric's deep voice rumbled with an angry undercurrent.

"*Prince* Eric." Mako's voice dripped with disdain, his demeanor morphing into a battle stance. "What a pleasure to see you aren't bottom-feeding anymore."

"Save your predatory ways for easier bait, chum."

"Watch your tone, freshwater. The Sharkanians will demolish your precious palace and everyone in it."

Eric's spear glowed darker at the threat. The animosity between Mako and Eric was a living creature, the tension palpable. If the mer-king had been killed by Sharkanians, there must be a deep chasm of hate between the two species. I wasn't ready to bear witness to the vicious battle that would surely ensue if the churning emotions weren't brought to check. Time to cool the tempers, if such was possible. In my experience, a little feminine intervention could work wonders. Or send men into a battle rage. I steeled my spine and put my hand on Eric's arm, urging him to lower his spear.

"Gentlemen, there's no need to go to war over me. Let's let the waters calm. Mr. Mako, thank you for ensuring my safety with your presence while Prince Eric was on official business. And for the lovely conversation. But now that he's returned, I'm in good hands. And I'm sure there are other fish in the sea to whom you can offer your protection."

A sense of the familiar slithered through me as I turned toward Eric so I could murmur in his ear. "Be nice to the sharks. They're not mean. They're misunderstood."

Where had I heard those words before?

Eric's gaze met mine, his brow furrowed in contemplation. He drew in a calming breath and nodded, his volatile expression calming. When I turned back to Mako, something passed over his face. An expression akin to admiration. Had he overheard my whisper?

Eric draped an arm around my waist, effectively laying claim to me. "Lady Ariel is as wise as she is beautiful, isn't she?"

His voice was steely, brooking no argument. He sounded ready to take on an entire Sharkanian army for me. My heart leapt at the realization that my merman was a total badass. Yet, he was also a man accustomed to leading with confidence and cooperation rather than sheer threat of power. The combination was both intoxicating and sobering.

Mako seemed to gauge the sincerity of Eric's tone for a moment, then bowed low to me. "Lady Ariel, you are indeed both wise and beautiful. I should hate the thought of you being forced to stay against your will."

Eric tensed, but I laughed. "Mako, I appreciate the concern. But I've been falling in love with Eric for weeks."

Oops! Had I said that out loud? The shock on Mako's face confirmed I had, and likely mirrored my own expression. He bowed again, his movements stiff and a look of betrayal in his eyes, then mumbled his condolences and swam away.

Two warm hands grasped my shoulder and turned me. Eric's expression was intense like earlier, his gray eyes burning into mine. "Really? You love me?"

I opened my mouth to deny the truth. After all, I'd fallen in love with an image and the idea of the perfect man I projected on to that image. I couldn't say the words he wanted, but neither could I pretend I felt nothing. "I...I'm not sure. I've stared at your image on a wall for weeks. I love the idea of the kind of man and lover you could be. And I love how I feel when I'm with you. Does that count?"

My heart raced, having been laid bare to him. Being stuck in a watery world I knew nothing about was added incentive to find things to love about him, but I had no problem swimming away from him if he turned out to be anything like my jerk exes. Fortunately, he was hitting all the non-jerk high points so far.

Eric's gaze held the same uncertainty I felt. "I understand, and I feel the same way about you. I've tried to convince myself fairy tales don't exist, but so far, you're a fantasy come true."

A closet dreamer just like me. Damned if that didn't make my heart flutter.

This sexy merman in front of me was better than any fantasy or projection. While my heart might have reservations, my body had none. It desired Eric—all of him—and hungered for more of what we'd begun earlier, if only to assure him of my attraction. "Eric, kiss me."

He didn't hesitate. His lips plundered mine, his arms wrapping around me and our tongues dueling. His tail flexed, propelling us through the water toward some destination, but I gave it no mind, lost as I was in the heat building in my core. Making love to him had been the center of most dreams these past few weeks and, even though I didn't have legs to wrap around him, I was primed to discover if making mer-love was even half as awesome as I'd imagined.

Soft strands caressed my back and sides, slipping across my skin and scales as his tail flicked again. I pulled away just enough to see we were in some sort of copse of tall grass, their broad leaves providing a modicum of privacy. "I thought aquatic life just went at it in the open."

"They do, but I'm not an exhibitionist and thought you might appreciate not having an audience for our first time."

"Our first time at what?" Yes, I wanted to have sex with him, but didn't want him assuming sex was a foregone conclusion. A girl had to play coy on occasion.

He pulled back, a lopsided smirk on his face that made my insides quiver. "Our first time at whatever we end up doing right now." He leaned in and kissed along my jaw, around the sensitive shell of my ear, and then down my neck to my shoulder.

By then, I was panting, clutching at the muscles on his back, wondering if it would be too forward to demand he fuck me right then and there.

"I want to kiss every inch of you." He murmured against my neck as his hands dove beneath the wafting hem of my shirt. I moaned when his hands clasped my waist, tickling my ribcage. His fingers splayed across my belly and back, tracing and kneading as if learning every detail of that part of my body. So close to the parts of my body I really wanted him to touch. His spoken desire to taste me hung, unaddressed, in the warm water between us. "Can I, Ariel? Lick you and taste you? Learn what makes you wriggle in ecstasy? Nibble on those spots that make you scream? Memorize you with my tongue? Bury my face in your glorious breasts and feast on your lovely little anemone?"

My answer came out as a keening moan with a desperate nod of my head. I gulped a mouthful of water so I could stutter. "Yes, and get to it before I harpoon you."

He pulled back on a chuckle. "I'll be the one harpooning you. But first, an appetizer."

With a flick of his hands, he whipped my shirt inside out over my face and arms, trapping me so I couldn't see or do anything. His mouth descended on mine again, kissing me fiercely through the fabric of the shirt, my naked breasts pressed to his unrelenting chest. He surged again, pushing me backward until I landed in a soft bed of plants, cushioning my body from behind as he blazed a trail of searing kisses to my chest. His hands released the shirt to palm my breasts, and I gasped. His large hands dwarfed their mass, plumping and squeezing, rolling my pearled nipples between his fingers. I flung off my shirt to watch as his mouth spread kisses from one nipple to the other, sucking and licking. I was mindless, arching against his assault on my breasts, clutching his head and clawing at his shoulders.

Just when I thought I might orgasm from that attention alone, Eric dipped further, kissing and licking across my ribs to my where my gills were. One glide of his tongue, and I moaned. Gills weren't ticklish like he'd claimed. They were an erogenous zone as sensitive as my clitoris had been. Before I could call him out for his deception, He slanted a mischievous grin my way. Cocky bastard knew exactly what he'd done.

He continued kissing down my belly, past the flowering anemone of my arousal, his mouth learning the shape of me just as he'd promised. Turns out the side of my tailfin where my knees might have been was an erogenous zone, and I flinched as he nibbled on the ticklish spines between the flesh of my caudal fin. Then he turned me over and kissed his return trip up, his hands roaming my front yet never quite touching where I wanted —needed more than I needed my next gulp of water—him to touch. His tongue swirled around a spot located where my—

"Holy mackerel, is that what I think it is?"

Eric chuckled, then tilted his head to the side to nip at the fleshy area. Then he swatted it before rubbing the slight sting away. "Yes, it is. Some things translate well from the bodies we once knew. Some don't." He circled his tongue around it again, and I moaned. "This is a more limited playground than before. But still fun to poke around."

Fun? More like amazing. If I'd known making out would be like this, we never would have left that first room.

A quick surge, and he proceeded to lick and nibble his way up my spine, pushing my face and breasts into the cushion of plants. Aside from the zaps and zings of pleasure Eric's kisses shot though me, the entire experience was freeing. I wasn't restricted by the cumbersome weight of my own body or his. The buoyancy of the water and the springy carpet beneath me made Eric's control overwhelming from a sensory standpoint without being physical. Even with his strength and command of my body, I felt embraced and safe. When he reached my neck, he flipped me over again, his body rubbing deliciously against mine, his breathing as labored as my own. "Ariel, your body is amazing. You better hang on to something because now I'm going after those frills."

I grasped at the nearby roots as he plunged straight to my core, the sweep of his tongue and lips against those engorged ruffles like fireworks in my brain. I cried out, breathless keening moans, and possibly his name and *God* mashed together. Then his tongue darted between those outer embellishments and into my slit, coaxing forth more mind-melting pleasure. It coursed through me until it exploded. I bent over him, clutching at his hair, both pushing him away and pulling him closer. When I was a quivering, boneless mass, he kissed his way back to my lips.

"Beautiful. And delicious." He murmured in between soft, tender kisses. "Sweetest sashimi."

A hard bulge pressed against my belly, a new, insistent sensation. I looked down and saw the bulge was attached to Eric. "Is that your…?"

His strained laugh held a hint of embarrassment. "Uh, yeah. It's one of those things that didn't translate well."

That was an understatement. His dick was huge, but unlike any I'd ever seen, and beautiful in its own weird way. Broad at the base—I doubted my hand could wrap around it—and tapering to a nubby point several inches later. It was a stubby pink tentacle drifting in the water like a fleshy frond of seaweed. Wait, the water current wasn't strong enough to account for all the wiggling his willy was doing, flicking and circling, reaching for my fronds.

"Uh, that thing is like a literal heat-seeking moisture missile. Are you in control of it?"

Eric barked a strangled laugh and rested his forehead against mine, his voice strained. "I'm a guy, Ariel. I'm in as much control of my erection as any man when he's holding such a desirable woman in his arms."

He pulled back, his brows furrowed in sincerity. "I

understand if you're freaked out. Believe me, so was I when I first saw it."

I cupped his face and brought his head in for a deep kiss. "I'm not freaked out. It's different, but not horrifying. In fact, I'm intrigued. How does this work for us?"

"I'm not sure." He whispered against my lips, his eyes closed as if he was afraid I might reject him. "I've never done this as a merman before."

All those merwomen out there in all the years he'd been here, and he'd never tried this with any of them? "Well, let's take it slow and see how well your eel fits in my anemone."

My body was primed to near-detonation, and I wanted to jump him like a trampoline. Instead, I grasped his shoulders while he held my hips steady. Our faces pressed together, we watched the scene at our pelvic areas unfold. Losing my virginity hadn't been this rife with nervous fascination and anticipation. The tips of his… was it still a dick?... spiraled a path around my pink fronds. Each gentle brush of his…penis…against them was a jolt of pleasure until my fingernails clawed his shoulders and I panted with need. My folds pulsed, beckoning him inside. When the tip finally eased past the fronds and into my slit, I moaned long and low.

This was more than mere penetration. Eric's sea snake hunted. We watched it enter me like a cautious cave-diver, pushing forward, retracting a step, testing along the sides for the way. I felt every flick and circle and surge, and the sensations fed my arousal until I thought I'd explode before he was fully inside me.

"Eric." I groaned his name, arching back. His lips locked on my nipples as my breasts floated upward. "This thing has a mind of its own and it's amazing."

"Give me a little credit." He grunted as our bodies met, his penis writhing deep inside me, my slit stretched wonderfully by the girth of his base. "My little head isn't doing anything my big head doesn't want it to."

"Well, whoever is in charge, they better not stop. I'm almost there."

Eric gripped my hips in his broad hands and kissed me deep, his tongue mimicking the plundering down below. Instead of the in and out thrusting and retreating I'd always known, our bodies remained connected. He swished his tail side to side with strong beats, each one pushing me against the soft carpet of vegetation beneath me, his flipping, undulating penis rubbing all my G-spots—apparently, I had several. I was soon a mindless, moaning, quivering lump of building ecstasy. Then the orgasm hit. It doused me like a white squall wave, sweeping me away from anything tangible and filling me with blinding light and fizzing bubbles of pleasure as if my entire body was a carbonated beverage shaken and left to explode. I screamed and convulsed until I collapsed with all the rigidity of a jellyfish.

Eric wrapped me in his arms, his worm still wiggling in my depths, his hot panting breaths against my cheek. His moans crested and he flipped me around so my back pressed against him. He roared my name into my hair and a flood of warmth spread across my lower back as he came.

We floated like that for several deep gulping breaths. I could barely form words and drifted in both mind and body. The pool of his cum expanded, and my greedy anemone pulsed, wafting the water—and cloudy stream of sperm—closer. I tensed, my gut clenching at the possible outcome if it were successful. Yet another thing that didn't translate well: my body's innate desire to reproduce usually happened deep inside where my not-ready-for-kids mind couldn't watch.

A strong surge shot us upward and away from the spreading jizz. When we were out of the danger zone, Eric whirled me back around then kissed me, long and with an ocean of feeling mirroring my own. "Sorry, there's no such thing as condoms here."

Fear of consequences and the future washed away, leaving a shiny spark of love glowing brighter than his spear. Blame it on the amazing orgasm, although I'd had some pretty good ones in the past and was always able to disassociate the physical from the emotional. The truth was, I was in love with this man. My artist's intuition knew Eric was worthy of all the tender emotions growing in my heart. Even the thought of a little merboy version of him swimming around me spurred a nugget of longing. I was ready to embrace a future in this watery world with this merman.

I cupped his face and kissed him back with all the love swelling in my chest. "Condoms or not, the sex was well worth the risk. And, despite my earlier claims, I do love you."

Shock struck him dumb, his jaw slack and his unblinking gaze holding mine. I laughed, which shoved him out of his spell. Then his expression turned serious. Had I said something wrong? He cleared his throat. "Follow me."

With only those two cryptic words to judge his mood by, he ushered me back to the palace and through several passageways. His body was tense, his motions brusque. What could his change of mood portend? Had I angered him with my confession? Had I crossed some unknown line, broken some unknown law? What man hears claims of love from a woman and doesn't try to wriggle out of the situation? Doesn't make lame excuses about prior commitments and *oh-gee-look-at-the-time*?

Or doesn't immediately return the sentiment?

Eric pulled me into a vacant room furnished only with a stone bench in the center and a kelp curtain along a far wall, not unlike the first room I'd been in. Or was it the same room? He turned to me and grabbed my hands, squeezing gently. His gaze roamed my face, like he was searching for words. Well, that made two of us.

"There's an Atlantian prophesy about two strangers from a

distant ocean who will bring a lasting peace between the merfolk and the Sharkanians."

"Good to know." What did that have to do with his weird behavior?

"I've never given it much credit, but the Atlantians believe it fervently. It's why so many of them were pointing to you in the marketplace."

I almost choked on my laugh. "They think I'm the fulfillment of some ancient prophesy?"

He shrugged. "Understand from their perspective. With you here, there are now two strangers from a distant ocean. Whether or not we can create any sort of peace with the Sharkanians is an entirely different challenge, and I'm not even saying we need to give it a try. But…you do seem to have a way with hungry beasts."

The smirk that lit his face made me blush, knowing he referred to his penis as equally as Mako. "Oh, I've only begun to have my way with your hungry beastie."

Eric smiled for a moment, but grew serious as quickly. "Try…" He cleared his throat and began again. "Try not to freak out."

Fear squeezed my heart. Those words were never a good sign. "Oooookaaaay."

His hands traced up my arms, leaving tendrils of warmth which wound their way to more intimate areas. When I expected him to move away, he flicked his tail and was flush against my body once more, his magic lips covering mine. It was an intense kiss, filled with desperation and need and something else I couldn't name.

As my womanly anemone begin to bloom, he pulled away and swam to the far wall. He grasped the edge of the kelp curtain, then hesitated. "They say this has been here for centuries. I've been fascinated since I first laid eyes on it, and have spent hours gazing at it."

With that cryptic introduction, he flicked the kelp aside. I gasped. Crafted with a myriad of tiny shells and stones were two merfolk posed in a loving embrace. The artist had been masterful, the figures nearly swimming off the wall in their realism. The merman was the exact likeness of Eric, down to the sexy smirk. In his arms was a beautiful mermaid with bright pink hair, sea green eyes, and a lush emerald-green tail. She bore a disconcerting likeness to me.

"That is an amazing work of art." My awe with the artist's skill bathed each word. I swum closer and ran my fingers over the details, admiring the craftsmanship.

"That is you."

"What? No, you're crazy. It's just a mermaid who looks like me."

"No, it's you. The turquoise flecks in the green eyes are the same as yours. The small paintbrush tattoo on the inside of the wrist. The dual beauty marks above your left eyebrow. Even the daisy, a flower which doesn't blossom in this watery world, tucked behind your ear."

As he spoke, he pointed to each feature which should be unique to me, but was also exactly reflected in the image. However, he didn't even see—or was too kind to mention—the biggest similarity. The mermaid's seashell-confined breasts were inconsistent in size, by nearly a full half cup. Why would the artist, who had so masterfully captured the texture of each tiny scale and individual strands of hair, accidentally craft one breast so much larger than the other? Unless...

"That's me?" I could barely believe the words I spoke.

"Yes." Eric traced a loving hand down the arm of the mermaid mosaic, then drifted to me. "But the image is nothing compared to the real thing."

He cupped my cheeks and brushed my lips with his, then deepened the kiss. Soon, we were both breathless and entangled in each other's arms, clutching and writhing. Eric pulled away enough to look at me.

"Ariel, I've gazed at that mermaid, imagining what a life with her would be like. You say you've spent weeks falling in love with me? I've spent years falling in love with you. Stay here in Atlantia with me."

"So, we can work together to create a lasting peace with the Sharkanians?"

"If you want. It will likely take years, if we can even succeed. But that's not what or why I'm asking you. As a man to a woman, I want you to be part of my world. Marry me."

I was a mermaid living in an ocean world. Unless I took a long walk off a short pier metaphorically speaking, since I couldn't drown anymore, I was going to spend the rest of my life here. My heart had already decided it belonged with Eric. My brain couldn't think of a better way to spend my life than with my fantasy-turned-real merman.

"There's just one problem, Eric." The hopeful expression on his face threatened to fall. I reached to twirl a lock of navy hair around my fingers and heaved a sighed. "How much I'm going to miss my lacy thong underwear."

His lips curved in the sexy smirk that made my fins quiver. He grasped my hips and pulled me against his growing erection. "I promise to do everything in my power to make you forget them."

"Ariel? Are you okay?" Eartha stepped through the entryway of the Morays' house. It hadn't fared very well during last night's storm. Ariel must not have been able to manually submerge and anchor it. The house floated, but barely and with a noticeable tilt to one side. The house was silent but for the strained hum of battered machinery. Had Ariel been injured? Or worse?

"Terra, be careful." She cautioned even as her daughter heedlessly skipped ahead into the main room. Chairs were tipped over and some of the lighter statues had upended as well. The groaning whir from the mechanical room indicated a problem. Something struggled to keep the house in its current condition, and it didn't sound healthy. Eartha called in to the community maintenance office. Perhaps Ariel had already notified them, but it didn't hurt to call again.

Wouldn't want the Morays' mansion to sink to the bottom of the lake. Especially before she found Ariel.

"Rod, this is Eartha from the market. I'm checking on the Morays' house. Their sitter said there was a problem with the mechanical room door, and it's in bad shape from the storms. Possibly a bladder leak. Could you send a repair unit? And an ambulance? I haven't found her yet, but my guess is she's probably injured."

Terra's excited voice sounded from the far side of the large living room. "Momma! Momma! The Pretty Mermaid!"

Eartha gulped down her fear. Was the poor thing dead? How would she explain this to her daughter?

As she rounded the couches, she saw Terra pointing at the fireplace and jumping with elation. The fireplace was fine, but on the nearby wall was a picture of a handsome merman. In one hand, he held a golden spear. His other hand was wrapped lovingly around the perfect likeness of Ariel. The image of the voluptuous pink-haired sitter—now with an emerald-green fishtail and large seashells covering her breasts—melted into the side of the strong merman, her face resting against his strong chest, a smile of utter contentment in her lips and eyes.

"Look, she's wearing my flower!" Terra giggled and clapped.

Sure enough, a dainty daisy peeked from between the floating strands of pink hair. How had she painted herself on the wall? And where was she now? Eartha turned to continue her search. "Help is coming, Terra. But we need to keep looking for Ariel."

"But I found her. She's right there." Terra waved her hand to the painting on the wall.

"Honey, that's not her. It's just a picture of her. Come back to the entrance so you don't get hurt and I'll keep looking for her."

Terra ran to the wall and placed her hands on either side of the image of Ariel and whispered loudly. "I was right about the sharks, wasn't I?" Then she turned and skipped across the room, waving behind her without a backward glance. "Have a nice life, pretty mermaid!"

～

KISS THE GIRL

Mako, a young Sharkanian General, knows there's more to life under the sea than hunting for food and waging war with the Atlantians. But he struggles against his own predatory nature until a gentle mermaid calms the savage hunger of his heart and tames his sharp bite.

I wandered aimlessly through the deep, calm waters of enemy territory. Well, not exactly *enemy* territory… this was the home of the merman who supposedly ruled over all the waters of Atlantia and its inhabitants. And these sprawling palace grounds were supposedly welcome to *all* the creatures of the sea, including my kind.

Tell that to the creatures I sluiced past.

The currents through the vibrant foliage and plentiful animal life covering the rolling coral beds surrounding the Atlantian palace were a gentle dance of serenity and harmony. Yet entire schools of fish darted away upon my approach. Crabs skittered. Anemone retracted. Even the merpeople gave me wide berth, not bothering to hide their wary glances.

I couldn't deny the urge to lift one side of my lips to show off my multiple rows of sharp, serrated teeth. Nor could I deny the dark satisfaction as I watched wary glances turn fearful.

While the palace grounds were a hunting-free zone in spite of the lush offering of tasty nibbles available, it was imperative I remind everyone what I was: cold-blooded hunter. Ruthless killer. Sharkanian.

As if they could ever forget it.

Not only did the sleek, powerful lines of my body, including the sharp angles of my tail and the telltale dorsal fin at my back, scream *predator*, but my mouth was filled with rows of teeth made to rend flesh from bone. What the average fish likely didn't know was that my brilliant blue coloring and the broad stripe of white on my chest tapering to a point at the base of my tail, meant I held the designated rank of General.

Meaning, among the feared Sharkanians, I was one of the select few to be feared the most.

All of my kind were feared. Feared and hated. Feared because of our predatory nature, as if we could change that any more than a jellyfish could grow a backbone. Hated because many years ago, we'd attacked and killed the ruling Atlantian King.

The battle had happened when I was just a pup on the cusp of training. So, I don't remember the reasons why my people had decided to rise up against the king after eons of living in relative peace. Maybe not *peace* so much as an uneasy civility, much like our current state of existence. All I really knew was that no one wanted to be around me or my Sharkanian brethren. Not that Sharkanians have any interest in mingling with these masses of prey. Except for me.

Not sure why I did.

Some part of me took a perverse joy in the palpable fear and occasional hostility which my presence on palace grounds provoked. Most creatures either fled immediately in fear or backed away while eyeing me for any suspicious moves. Fine by me. I didn't need their approval or their friendship. As long as the respect I was due swam in tandem with that fear and suspicion, I wouldn't blink an eye.

Heh-heh. *Blink an eye.* That was funny. Because I was Sharkanian. And we didn't have any eyelids. We couldn't blink. We...

Okay, not really that funny. But what could I say? I was Sharkanian. We weren't known for our sense of humor. We were obviously known for attacking and killing and inspiring fear.

Of all the merpeople I'd ever interacted with, only one hadn't been afraid of me. The pink-haired mermaid I'd happened upon awhile back. She'd been oddly alone, resting against a cluster of rocks, casually wafting her fingers and water over her exposed genitalia, the silky fronds bright pink with arousal. The sight had been the most erotic of my life, which was saying something because sea creatures were never coy about sex, especially Sharkanians. We fucked wherever, whenever, and whomever we wanted. An ovulating female could always choose from a long line of lovers gnashing their teeth to have a go. Maybe that was why finding a lone mer so obviously turned on and yet without a partner had been such a novelty. I'd been about to offer my assistance in finding her release, when *he* had interrupted.

Prince Eric.

My mouth filled with bitter flavor, like I'd chewed a clam shell, thinking of that bit of chum. He was the mer who'd replaced the Atlantian king we Sharkanians had assassinated all those years ago. Sharkanian opinion considered Prince Eric to be leagues better than the former ruler, but that didn't mean we were complacent, unquestioning supporters. It simply wasn't in our nature to follow blindly.

My personal opinion of Prince Eric was further skewed because he'd been a clasper-blocker, showing up and claiming the pink-haired mer before I could. Not that I'd truly had a chance; she had quickly admitted she was in love with the Atlantian ruler.

Both Prince Eric and the female mermaid—Princess Ariel, he had called her—were unusual mers. Their facial features were more defined. More rounded, their lips larger, their eyes set closer together on their faces. Princess Ariel's caudal fin was full and luscious. She carried two enormous air bladders on her chest, which was bizarre, considering most fish and merpeople carried theirs internally.

At first glance, Eric and Princess Ariel's facial features were disconcerting. But I rather liked their diversity. Maybe it meant good tides for the antagonistic relations between the Atlantians and the Sharkanians. Or maybe it meant yet another species that despised my kind.

Pain burst in my shoulder, yanking me downward and flipping me around. My skin burned, possibly torn from the impact of whatever had hit me.

"Go home, Sharkanian scum! You're not welcome here!" Someone jeered from above me, peeking over the edge of a jutting cliff and waving a chunk of basalt that likely resembled what had just smashed into me.

Which meant it hadn't been an accident.

Spume. A gang of merteens glared at me from atop the small coral cliff. Merteens were the worst. Atlantian adults in body only. Trying to prove themselves tough against a Sharkanian, yet hiding in the safety of numbers and assuming the high ground gave them the advantage.

Honestly, I had been just like them, anxious to prove myself brave. All my Sharkanian brethren had at that age. But I doubted these merteens would take such an admission on my part as anything other than a sign of weakness.

One strong whip of my tail, and I debunked their assumption they had any positional advantage. I swiftly crested the top of the cliff and sneered at them. Seven of them, and they all flinched, their gills flaring in fear when I flashed my predator's smile.

I could have chosen violence—no one would be surprised if I had—but instead, I decided to have a little fun. "Go home? Why would I do that when I see children who obviously got separated from the rest of their school? I should escort you back. You know, to ensure your safety."

They trembled, drifting closer to one another as if a tight-knit cluster would protect them should I decide to attack. Someone at the back of the bundle must have pushed at the largest of them, shoving him toward me as either their representative, their hero, or their sacrifice.

I crossed my arms and waited for him to gather up his courage. His thin-lipped mouth, just like mine except mine hid hundreds of serrated teeth, turned down in a quivering frown. Then he puffed out his chest, lifted his head defiantly, and huffed a laugh as if he'd battled worse than me and come out the victor.

I doubted he'd ever battled even a sea slug, much less been victorious against it.

"One lone Sharkanian against seven of us?" The merteen swallowed past his false bravado. "Those aren't very good odds."

"You are correct." I dropped my arms to my side and flicked my tail enough to glide closer, nearly within reach. The merteen lost some of his already-dull greenish-gray color. "Those aren't very good odds for you. Perhaps you should be smart and retreat instead."

His large eyes narrowed, his nictitating lens contracting over his eyes and giving him a mutinous appearance.

Well, *spume*. Blame bravado, peer pressure, or plain

stupidity, but this mer wasn't backing down. And his act of fearlessness emboldened his friends. They tensed for a fight, reaching for the assortment of coral spikes and shell knives they'd secured to their bodies for such occasions. Knives that were barely sharp enough to break my skin or long enough to hit anything vital. Still, the seven of them looked ready and willing to prove themselves against me.

As if I wasn't evolution's perfect weapon of death.

A firm hand landed on my shoulder, the one that still stung from a so-called falling boulder. I turned my black eyes to the lead mer who had brazened to draw close enough to touch me. He still smelled of fear, but not enough to avoid making stupid decisions. I forced my motions to be as slow and unthreatening as a Sharkanian could make them. I didn't even flash my teeth. We were still on palace grounds, and no way would I risk the tenuous truce between the mers and my kind over a tussle with few dumb teens.

I was a General. I was better than that.

"*We* don't need to retreat." Their leader declared boldly. "We have knives. You have nothing."

I grit my jaw, my rows of teeth grinding together. Oh, how mistaken he was. I longed to eviscerate them all for foolishly standing against me. For provoking me.

But rather than attack, I merely jerked my shoulder from the grip of the mer in front of me. He hissed in pain as my dermal denticles scraped against the tender flesh of his palm and shredded the webbing between his fingers. Even my skin was a weapon, my tiny scales as sharp as my teeth.

"Oops. Sorry." I nodded toward the merteen's hand he now cradled, hating that I had to pretend it was an accident. "My skin is a bit abrasive when I'm rubbed the wrong way. You might want to get that looked at."

The leader was too shocked about his hand to respond, but the rest of his gang practically vibrated with rage. Their tensing muscles created minute ripples in the waters around us, which the electroreceptor pores at my temples sensed easily. Again, because I was evolution's perfect weapon of death, those pores were a physical advantage that helped me find prey. They also gave me special advantage in battle.

But this wasn't battle. This was stupid.

If only I could convince the merteens of that. They seemed intent on rushing headlong into a fight with me, likely assuming their numbers meant something. I was either going to have to retreat or violently disabuse them of their ignorance. In the mers' current state of agitation, I doubted they'd listen to reason. They'd likely assume any attempt to verbally diffuse the situation with them would be a sign of weakness on my part. As a Sharkanian, and a General at that, I'd never back down from a fight, which meant my only real choice was a show of physical force. I'd have to injure—or worse—the mers to get my point across. Unfortunately, seven injured mers would invite the attention of other opportunistic predators. And the pissy little chums would probably go cry to their brooders, who would complain to the mer authorities, and it might even get so far as to Prince Eric.

I gnashed my teeth. The prince was not high on my favorite fish list. And if he was even half as volatile as the previous king had supposedly been, this little skirmish with idiotic merteens could quickly blow up into another war between Sharkania and Atlantia.

I wasn't afraid of war. But I didn't want to be the cause of it. Nor did I want these reckless teens to be the reason I might cause one.

Spume! Daring the anger of Ursule the sea witch wasn't this rife with consequences, each one worse than the next and none of them acceptable. I'd rather tempt the dangers of a hydrothermal vent than be here.

My spores sensed the growing agitation of the mers, their

muscles tensed for attack and their heartbeats racing. I stilled, my own muscles lax but my predator brain sharp and ready to react instantly, my actions dependent on theirs. The water along my gill slits paused, like time stopped, slowed, this watery world suspended in anticipation before one of us moved and nothing would ever be the same again.

"You boys look like you're having fun." A musical voice cut through the tension surrounding us, and the distraction sucked the anger away faster than a tidal current. We all looked to the source, and I caught my breath.

Princess Ariel approached us, heedless of the danger of simmering violence. Her pink hair floated around her like a school of devoted remora. She had traded out the awkward, figure-hiding garment she'd worn the day I first met her, and now wore two large shells over her external air bladders. She was built too strangely to be considered attractive, but she carried herself with the confidence of her position as the future Atlantian queen. Perhaps she could broker a little bit of peace between the merteens and me.

Or, perhaps she'd prove herself just as anti-Sharkania as all the others. I clenched my fists, refusing to be surprised if she did, even though some deep-down naïve part of me hoped there was a chance she wouldn't.

"Princess Ariel." I greeted with a bow, forcing my voice to be calm. "It is a pleasure to see you again."

Would she remember me? Would she acknowledge if she did? The merteens looked between us, their expressions leaping between anger and awe, suspicion and enchantment. Waiting to see where their emotions should land, dependent on how Princess Ariel responded to me.

I teetered on the ledge of a chasm that would either destroy me or save me. And I hated it. No one, even royalty, should have so much power over another.

"Yes, it's good to see you again, Mako." Princess Ariel's full lips lifted with happiness and she laughed. "I'm very glad the circumstances are different than the last time."

Was she actually referring to the fact I'd found her pleasuring herself?

The teens gaped at how easily Princess Ariel spoke to me, as if we were old friends. Then she looked between all of us and raised one of the dark stripes situated above her eyes. "Although once again, you seem to be ruffling feathers."

Feathers? I blinked at her, not understanding what she meant. What were feathers?

She laughed even louder and waved her hands. "Oops, sorry! I'm still learning the ways of your water world. That was a reference you wouldn't know, but I'm basically pointing out the fact that all of you were just about to fight each other."

Then she speared us all with a look that bordered on scolding, crossing her arms over her air bladders. The teens cowered. One even squirted a string of feces that floated around their tails like a lamprey looking for a host. I was not afraid. Instead, I fought a wave of defiance that threatened to drown me from her words and tone.

I was no child. I had done nothing to warrant a reprimand. I—

"Why are you seven here?" She turned to the teens with her question.

Their leader thrust the hand he still coddled toward her. "This Sharkanian attacked us, My Lady, leaving my hand shredded beyond repair. I demand you have him arrested for his crime."

Before I could defend myself with the truth, Princess Ariel palmed the teen's injured hand and examined it. We held our collective breaths, waiting for her to say something. Again, I hated that she yielded so much influence. When she finally nodded, my heart sank and I watched the collective look of triumph spread through the teens.

She looked at the teen whose hand she still held. "I've gotten worse scrapes from brushing against the palace walls. You're fine."

The teen stared at her in shock. She crossed her arms over her air bladders again and glared at him. "And I'm not buying your accusation that Mako attacked you. In case you haven't noticed, he's a Sharkanian. They are a lot of things, but timid is not one of them. If he'd attacked you like you claimed, you'd be crying over far more serious injuries than a tiny scrape on your hand. Assuming he left you alive to cry at all."

The teen opened his mouth to either object or make up another lie, but Princess Ariel was already shaking her head to stop him. "Which means, the only crime I see here is the obvious fact you put your hands on someone—specifically Mako—without their consent."

My fins nearly fell off.

Princess Ariel had not only swept away the mer's accusation against me, but had also turned the tide to make it seem like the merteen was actually in the wrong. She had defended me. Defended a Sharkanian, the same species everyone assumed were savage war-mongering bottom-feeders with nothing else on their minds but to kill and eat, not necessarily in that order.

One of the other teens spoke up. "Princess Ariel, you are right, we did lay a hand on him. But this is a Sharkanian, and they are savage, war-mongering bottom feeders."

Point proven. Too bad I was incapable of rolling my eyes.

"I am well aware of what everyone thinks of the Sharkanians." Princess Ariel's voice held an edge as sharp as my teeth. "Don't assume I agree with it."

"W-we were merely trying to get him to leave so no Atlantian would be harmed by him."

I almost laughed at that. I'd swum the palace grounds for half the day before these teens tried to run me off. I would have laughed, but my shoulder still ached from their attempt to get me to leave.

Princess Ariel didn't laugh either. "The palace grounds are welcome to *all* the creatures of the sea. You know this. You also know you're supposed to be in school right now. So run along and return to your studies. I *will* follow up with your teachers to make sure you make it there."

"But Princess Ariel." One of them interjected. "That would leave you alone with the Sharkanian."

"Good observation." Her voice held a note of exasperation. "I will be safe with Mako. You should be more concerned about yourselves after I bring this episode up to Prince Eric."

On a collective gasp, seven merteens zipped away, fear in their eyes.

Fear put there by a mild threat from their future queen. Fear I hadn't been able to instill in them. Had I lost my touch? Who did I have to fillet to restore my reputation?

"Perhaps you shouldn't trust so blindly that you are safe alone with me, Princess Ariel." I snarled.

"I have heard all the terrifying rumors, Mako. But I think deep down, there is more of a hero in you than a villain." Princess Ariel smiled as she turned to me. "That said, does trouble *always* follow you?"

"My reputation precedes me." Apparently not really, but I shrugged as if it did and I didn't care about that fact. The slight motion made me grimace, my injured shoulder aching.

Her expression morphed into concern. "Are you hurt? Let me see."

With a shake of my head, I pulled back, turning my injured shoulder further from her view. Showing weakness could get you killed in my world, and a Sharkanian showing weakness to an Atlantian was a fate worse than death. Princess Ariel might be an ally—or, at least, not entirely an enemy—but a lifetime of training demanded I not show her just how much damage those merteens had inflicted.

"I am fine, Princess Ariel. But thank you for your assistance with the teens." I refused to be a victim. I was a cold-blooded killer; a little bonk with a rock wouldn't slow me down.

She cocked her head to the side and one of her face stripes lifted again. "You know, Mako, those teens might have an opportunity to present their side of the story to Prince Eric. In my former world, inhabitants would often tell what we called *fish tales.* Meaning the details that made them look better were always exaggerated, and the details that made them look bad were minimized or conveniently forgotten. I have a feeling those teens will tell some whopper fish tales. But if you came to tell your side of the story, or showed me what they did to you, that could provide a check and balance to their tales. And might help battle the unfair Sharkanian stereotype."

Every cartilaginous fiber in my body balked at the suggestion. Tell Prince Eric my side of the interaction with the teens? Show him the scrapes on my shoulder? Plead with him to be fair in his judgement?

I didn't trust anyone enough for that.

Princess Ariel might have enough influence over her fiancé to get him to open his mind to the possibility I was innocent, but everything I'd been taught to believe affirmed it would be disastrous. Bad for me, personally, and bad for all of Sharkania. A large bite of our power stemmed from our reputation. And our reputation inspired fear. If the Atlantians saw us as victims— stopped being afraid of us, or worse, started feeling sorry for us —that would doom my kind. We'd have to become even more cold-blooded and blood-thirsty just to maintain some semblance of respect.

And by doing so, we might begin another war with Atlantia.

There was no way to avoid catastrophe for Sharkania if I gave in to her request to see my injury. So, I shook my head. "I appreciate your concern, Princess Ariel. But I think it's best that I return to my home."

She met my even gaze for a moment before nodding in

understanding. "Please don't be a stranger among our waters, Mako. Familiarity might not mean the end of Sharkania, as you believe."

"If anyone can turn the tides, it would be you, My Lady." I let the current pull me away, but did not turn my back to her until the distance was too great to see her expression any more. The extent of my injury safe from her curious eyes, I turned and sliced toward the Sharkanian borders, my heart erratic in my chest.

Too many complex thoughts swarmed in my head. Had I made the right decision? Should I stop swimming palace grounds? Should I swim palace grounds even *more*? Would familiarity breed comfort, or would my presence continue to agitate? Was it even possible to exist among the Atlantians, given their abject fear and hate of my kind, much of which we'd cultivated and some of which was grounded in truth? Could I leverage Princess Ariel's sympathy to Sharkanian advantage? What actions could I take to strengthen Sharkanian-Atlantian relations that wouldn't invite my kind to attempt a conquest? Was it even possible for our people to live in peace?

And why would I even want peace? I was a Sharkanian General; I'd been raised and trained for war.

I slowed and ran my fingers through my short hair, gritting my teeth against the sharp stab of pain in my shoulder from the move. I should want war, not peace. But my gut told me there had to be a way for all of us to live together. At the very least, my kind should be able to swim among the others without being physically or verbally accosted.

Atlantians judged us immediately, assuming we were thoughtless and indiscriminate killers. Which we were, during a feeding frenzy when our innate nature and eons of evolution took over. But we were also much more.

How to get the Atlantians to see this, without sacrificing Sharkanian strength and pride in our heritage?

There was so much at stake, but it required a skilled fin to handle.

Spume. There wasn't anything skilled about me. I was a lethal hunting and killing lifeform, and none of that took any particular skill, only evolutionary advantage such as strength, speed, agility, and rows of razor teeth. Even Sharkanian fighting tactics had evolved from generations of experience fine-tuned to its most efficient and effective levels. All we really ever had to do was throw numbers into the mix. Get enough Sharkanians into a designated area, allow our reputation to terrify the surrounding fish into a panic, add a drop of blood, and let our natural instincts take care of the rest.

I scrubbed my hand down my face in hopeless frustration and resumed my journey home.

Once I'd crossed into Sharkanian waters, it didn't take long to draw a crowd, and soon a shiver of fellow Sharkanians four-bodies deep surrounded me. Injuries would do that in our world. Injuries or any other sign of weakness. Sometimes I wondered who was a bigger Sharkanian enemy: Atlantians or our own kind.

A number of sharks merely swam along, I guess waiting for me to either die or possibly toss them bits of my own flesh. But in typical Sharkanian hunting habit, most circled tightly around me. No small feat since I swam at a pretty swift pace. Several approached from below, making their presence known where my soft, vulnerable underbelly was exposed. They didn't get close enough to do anything about it, but they simply made sure I was aware of the danger.

As if I didn't know how Sharkanians behaved when hunting prey.

I swam as if I hadn't care in the world. As if my rank of General was enough to hold these lower-level chums in check. Unfortunately, that power was tenuous at best, and often disregarded when easy prey was near.

I flashed them my teeth. I was no one's prey.

Before I reached our stronghold, my older brother, Glut, stopped me.

"What happened, Mako?" He crossed his arms over his broad chest, his uniform sash stiff with weaponry. Weaponry he didn't need, but was required to wear when on duty. His imposing figure intimidated most and impressed the rest, but the bulky uniform slowed him down. I could easily zip past him and into the stronghold without answering his question.

Which would only result in a thrashing once he found and cornered me.

I stopped to face him rather than appear frightened by running away. As a fellow General, I did not run away from anything.

"What do you mean, *what happened*, brother?" I forced bored innocence in my voice. My shoulder ached like I'd been pricked by a venomous spiny urchin, but I'd rather be flayed than admit I was in pain. Especially with such a large and opportunistic audience.

Sharkanians didn't show weakness. Ever.

Glut sighed, the only sign he saw past my pretense. "You smell of blood. Your own blood. What happened?"

I tried to shrug away his concern, but he grabbed my arm and whipped me around to see my shoulder for himself. Before I could explain—or lie—he continued. "Why does your shoulder look like you scratched an itch against a barnacle bed?"

If we didn't have an audience, I might have whispered the truth to him. But I didn't dare look weak. Nor did I dare insinuate an Atlantian—or seven—had anything to do with my injury, and thus spawn another war. "Rogue current smashed me against some coral."

A few onlookers snorted with disdain, which wasn't surprising. Being pushed into a coral reef *by water* was an impressive level of incompetence, even if rogue currents were notoriously volatile.

Glut frowned at me. "I'm surprised a Sharkanian General with your level of training and skill could be so injured by a current."

"Believe me, I was surprised as well." I drifted back around to face him, forcing arrogance and a nuance of surprised offense into my voice. "So, you can imagine the strength of the current which injured this trained and skilled General."

My brother stared at me for several moments. Then nodded and clamped a large hand on my good shoulder. "It must have been powerful indeed. Let's get you some food."

We turned together to swim through the stronghold entrance, both of us ignoring the disappointment of the onlookers we left behind.

You'll get no entertainment from me.

Lower ranked Sharkanians such as our audience were little better than unprincipled barracuda, quick to turn on friend or foe, hungry for violence even among our brethren. Some of this was nature, but most was because few were encouraged to control our instinctive impulses during our formative years. Like most fish in the sea who leave their children to fend for themselves, Sharkanian mothers give birth and then swim away, leaving their progeny with little but our instincts to guide us.

Because of all this, there were few Sharkanians I trusted. And fewer with whom I'd share my belief we should garner a stronger peace with Atlantia. That we should look for ways to integrate among the rest of the ocean's creatures.

Actually, I had yet to share those thoughts with anyone.

Glut and I reached the central dining room, currently empty because mealtime had passed. The stronghold was carved out of a dark ocean mountain which had risen from the fissure of an enormous deep-sea trench. Unlike the Atlantian palace which soared up from the sea floor to heights some claimed reached above the waves, the Sharkanian stronghold did not rise above the surrounding ocean floor more than a couple levels. Instead, hundreds of training rooms, weapons storage, and communal sleeping rooms had been carved into its depths. Even though many Sharkanians chose to live outside of our stronghold, the central dining room was the heart of our mountain and our land, created to hold hundreds of Sharkanians at a time for meals or meetings. Unlike the high vaulted ceilings of the Atlantian throne room, where sounds bounced around as a cacophonous symphony, this room had low ceilings that muted echoes. All conversations—even those directed to a vast audience—were cozy, intimate interactions that felt additionally private. As if we all shared closely-guarded secrets.

Perhaps that wasn't too far from the truth.

Glut turned to me again once we'd situated a safe distance from any curious eyes and ears. He crossed his arms. "Okay, what really happened."

I tried to read his expression and body language to determine how much of the truth to tell, if any. But he was as expressionless as any of our kind. Unsmiling, large black eyes known for their death stare, and the unruffled demeanor that meant either he felt truly relaxed and unthreatened, or he was poised for attack.

Spume. All his Sharkanian training made it impossible for me to utilize mine to gauge his intention.

I sighed, water passing quickly over my gills. Truth, it would be, then. At least part of it. "A few dumb mer teens dropped a block of basalt on me in an effort to scare me away from the Atlantian palace grounds."

Glut growled, gnashing his rows of teeth. "That is cause to start a war."

I waved away his declaration. "Really? A few stupid teens thinking they have what it takes to stand up to a Sharkanian

General, and you propose war? Were we any less eager to prove ourselves at that age?"

Glut's signature frown deepened. "A few teens will turn into thousands if they aren't put in their place."

"What makes you think I didn't put them in their place?"

He stared at me expectantly. "Well? Did you?"

I crossed my arms to match his stance and smirked. Too bad my self-restraint with the mer teens would not be seen as admirable. So I smeared the truth a bit as I chuckled at the memory. "Well, one of them shit himself, they were so scared. Does that count?"

He could pull all my teeth but I'd never admit Princess Ariel was the real reason for why the teens were put in their place. Even her show of support and declaration that Sharkanians were welcome on palace grounds would be wrongfully construed as weakness on my part. We Sharkanians shouldn't need permission. We shouldn't require royal intervention or support. The fact that it had happened to me—whether I requested it or not—would be viewed harshly by my brethren. Even my brother.

"How?" Glut asked. "How did you put them in their place?"

I drifted back just enough to let him know I did not appreciate the question. If he weren't my brother, that question could have been reason enough to fight, if only to put *him* in *his* place, no matter that he was older and larger than me. Instead, I glared. "By my mere presence. It's easy enough to throw a rock at me, but to face me while I flashed my teeth was more than they could handle. They high-tailed it back to their school."

Glut stared at me for several moments, as if trying to determine the truth of my words. Finally, he nodded once. "Okay. As long as they were properly punished for their actions."

"Of course. Can't let the stupidity of youth go without proper punishment." Hopefully, the bitterness I felt did not seep into my voice.

"I care more that they do not toss another block of basalt at you." He sighed in frustration, a sound he'd made many times as I'd grown up. "Although maybe they'd hit you on the head and knock some sense into you."

I growled. "Maybe if you didn't always chase after lone Atlantians and pretend you're going to eat them, they wouldn't try to throw rocks at me."

He looked only mildly penitent, shrugging. "But it's my favorite pastime. They make such funny faces when they scream." Then his expression sobered. "But perhaps steer clear of Atlantia the next time you go for a swim. Your presence as a lone Sharkanian lures them to attack, yet you do not want the war their actions should bring."

My hands fisted at my side as my gut hollowed. I heard the meaning behind his words. Glut thought I was reckless for swimming Atlantian grounds. He thought I was spineless for wanting to avoid war.

Bitterness definitely seeped into my voice. "I am not as weak as you obviously believe I am. Good day, brother."

I turned to swim away as he muttered something under his breath. His words didn't register until I was nearly to my barracks, and their meaning was an air bubble in my veins.

"You aren't weak, brother. But you can't turn the tide alone."

The pain in my shoulder was agony. The shredded flesh trailed like seaweed in the water as I swam and the exposed tissue stung from our salty environment. My wound would eventually heal, but it wouldn't be pretty. Which didn't matter; Sharkanians preferred the scars of strife to beauty. Our scars were badges of honor. Our injuries were testimonies to our strength. And if we died from them, we could die with pride.

Not sure my injuries would count as any of that.

I'd left the stronghold and Sharkanian waters to be alone and away from the judging eyes of my kind, my brother included.

While I did not consciously abide by his request to avoid swimming in Atlantian waters, I found myself in the barren waters of the Wastes, if only to allow for uninterrupted time to think.

The more I contemplated our own harsh Sharkanian culture, the more I realized Glut was right about not being able to convince the Atlantians to see us as anything but savage killers. And the more enraged I became.

So filled with rage that I wanted to savagely kill something.

I paused against a rocky outcropping to take some deep, calming breaths. And to eat the chunk of tuna I'd harvested. As I swam, I'd come across an elderly tuna whose swim bladder had deteriorated so he could barely remain upright, much less swim forward with any agility. He couldn't keep up with his school, which had left him behind, alone and vulnerable.

Yes, I'd been angry enough to kill something, but not like this.

Then he had turned his despondent eyes to me. I'd seen that same look many times in my life. The look of knowing death was on the horizon and the fish was helpless to stop its approach. The only power they held was a desperate choice of when and in what form that death could take. Meaning, a swift, relatively painless death by a Sharkanian who had been evolved and trained to dole it out.

So much better than the agony of a failing body, starvation, and being slowly eaten alive by the sharp nibbles of smaller fish.

With a slight nod to acknowledge the elderly fish's unspoken plea, I dealt a killing hit with my tail, snapping his backbone. It was the quickest death I could provide. And then I helped myself to a chunk of his side as my payment. Some might condemn us for it, but Sharkanians dined on the weak and the dead.

Truth be told, most aquatic creatures ate other aquatic creatures. Why Sharkanian nature to do the same was used against us—to label us as somehow more violent and reprehensible because of our eating habits—I would never understand.

"Leave me alone!" A feminine voice drifted from below. Her words were firm, but her tone carried a thread of alarm that triggered my electroreceptor pores. Sight unseen, I already knew she trembled in fear.

Curious, I drifted past the outcropping and to the edge of a culvert where beds of shallow kelp hid me so I could watch the drama below unfold. Three mermen had cornered a mermaid against an inset of the culvert wall. Unlike the unremarkable green-gray color of the mermen, the scales of the mermaid's rounded, blunt-finned tail shimmered silvery-white, with several traverse bands of the faintest discoloration. Her face was pale but lovely, even as her expression was pinched with worry. She was slender, and wore nothing, not even the seashells many merwomen chose to band across their chest. This frightened mermaid was plastered against the unyielding stone of the culvert wall with no way to escape without first moving *closer* to her adversaries in such a manner they could easily—purposefully —misconstrue as an invitation.

"Leave you alone?" One of the mermen drifted closer, resting his forearm against the wall and leaning toward the mermaid in a casual yet direct refusal to abide her demand. "But you're such a tasty treat. If we left you alone out here in the wastes, something horrible might happen to you."

"Yeah, we're just trying to keep you safe." One of the other mermen leered at her.

The third mer licked his lips and palmed the slit in his tail where his penis had already begun to emerge, the tip wriggling like a tentacle with a mind of its own. "Who knows what sort of terrifying predator would happen upon you if we left?"

The first mer traced a finger from the mermaid's throat down to the edge of her tail scales. She shuddered and tried to flinch away from his touch, but there was nowhere for her to go. His smile turned triumphant, with a healthy dose of lust. "You wouldn't want to get eaten alive by a Sharkanian, would you?"

The mermaid lifted her chin in defiance even as she trembled in fear. But before she could respond, I had whipped over the kelp beds to the culvert and drifted down behind the mermen.

"You're terribly misinformed. We Sharkanians prefer our meals injured or already dead." The mermen jerked around to face the intruder who dared interrupt their hunting. They recoiled in terror when they realized they'd conjured a Sharkanian by their words. I nodded to indicate the mermaid. "We don't corner and taunt our prey."

Chunk of flesh still in my hand, I ripped off another bite as the mermen simply stared at me, their mouths open as if they might actually regret their life's decisions. I shrugged. "The only thing horrible that might happen to this lovely mermaid is you three."

I would choke on my tuna before I called them *predators*.

The first mer rallied, waving his hand to indicate me. "See? This is why you should let us protect you. So you don't end up as dinner."

Had he not heard me say she was safe from that?

The mer tried to wrap his arm around the mermaid, but she managed the wriggle away from his grasp. He glared at her for making him look like a fool, but his glare withered when I speared him with a scowl.

"That's an interesting choice of words coming from a mer who just called her a tasty treat." I caught the mermaid's gaze so she would know I spoke directly to her. "I would hate the thought of you being forced to accept their companionship against your will."

Her face softened with relief and the tension in her body whooshed out like a squid's propulsion. Her faint bands of discoloration deepened to a rich, dark blue as the fear that gripped her eased.

72

Odd. The presence of my kind never relaxed anyone.

I continued. "Tell me to leave and I will do so immediately, but if these three are bothering you, I will help you get rid of them."

She glanced at each of the three mermen, eyes wide as if expecting them to pounce on her regardless of my threat. When she turned her gaze back to me, that telltale sign of worry calmed. Then her lips lifted in a shy smile, and my heart exploded.

Had I offered to rid her of the three annoying mers? I would battle all of Atlantia for that sweet upturn of her lips.

"Thank you for your help." She spoke to me, her soft voice more musical than even the king's royal orchestra, which I'd only ever heard from a distance as I wandered the dunes at the edge of palace grounds. Sharkanians never ventured into crowds unless we wanted to incite a panic. Still, the music had made me smile as its lilting melodies drifted along the current. As pleasing as that experience had been, it paled in comparison to my body's current response. This mermaid's voice fizzed along my limbs and down my back like the tickling bubbles of a deep-sea vent. I caught my breath against the unusual, though strangely enjoyable, sensation.

Then she blinded me with the full force of her smile, and I forgot how to pass water along my gills. "I would very much like to be rid of these three. I've asked them repeatedly to leave me alone and they refuse."

"B-but, we're just trying to keep you safe." The second one objected.

The first one reached for her again, but she evaded his touch. The third one glared at me, his muscles tensed for attack.

"How do we know you won't try to eat her?" The first one narrowed his eyes at me.

I certainly didn't want to eat her as if she were a chunk of dead tuna, but I did have a desperate urge to know how she tasted. I wanted to run my tongue along her bold stripes. Wanted to gently nibble on her sensitive spots to hear what sounds she might make.

Would those sounds also tingle along my nerves?

Sharkanians rarely paid attention to other sea creatures with the exception of what they could provide in the way of sustenance. So why was I so intrigued by this mermaid?

No answer to this question bouncing around my goldfish brain, I threw the mer's words back at him. "How does she know you won't attempt the same?"

The mermen gasped at my comment as if I'd offended them, and I shrugged. "I might be a mindless creature of violence, but even I can see she is uncomfortable with the three of you."

They all looked at her for confirmation she shouldn't need to give, which allowed me the opportunity to drift closer to the third one in case this interaction devolved into violence. She fisted her hands at her side and frowned, looking at each of the three mermen who were willfully as dense as a sunfish. "For the last time, I do not want your help. I do not need your help. I am not your responsibility. Leave me alone."

"You heard her. Leave." I murmured in the third mer's ear, his distracted attention allowing me to advance dangerously close to him. He realized immediately I was close enough to kill with a single snap. On a yelp, he swung around, fist raised to make contact with my jaw. But I blocked his punch, then bent into a twist and thumped his unprotected belly with my tail, launching him against the culvert wall as he *oofed* and crumpled from the impact.

"Hey, you bottom-feeder!" The second mer pulled a knife of sharpened shale and stabbed toward me. I trapped his wrist in my hands, twisting and forcing him to jab himself under the chin with his own weapon, sharp side down so he didn't bleed.

The last thing I needed was to draw an audience of fellow

bottom-feeders to escalate this tussle into a frenzy. Or fall into one myself.

The first mer bellowed something as he joined the fray, but I blocked him with the body of his friend, who I still held with a knife to his throat. The second mer grunted in pain from the contact, then I yanked him closer and bashed his face with my forehead, stunning him.

He floated to the ground and I turned my focus to the first mer. Terror transformed him from lecherous predator to trembling prey, and he backed away as I advanced on him until he was trapped in the same inset he'd cornered the lovely mermaid in.

Lifting my lips to showcase my teeth in a menacing way that often stopped the heart of my prey, I braced my forearm against the wall and leaned closer. "What's wrong? You're such a tasty treat, I'd hate for something horrible to happen to you out here in the wastes."

His frightened whimpers made me smile broader, and I dragged a finger down his chest like he had the mermaid. "You wouldn't want to get eaten by a Sharkanian, would you?"

The mer shook his head, his terrified gaze never leaving mine. His chest heaved and the warm current of water circling my tail proved he'd just pissed himself. Without his friends at his back to help terrorize a helpless mermaid, his courage streamed away as quickly as his urine. Even the small mermaid hadn't been this petrified, and she'd faced three intimidating mermen with less-than-noble intentions.

I fisted his hair and yanked his head back, exposing his neck as if I might slash it open with a single bite. The mer whimpered, but I merely snarled. "Now you also know what it's like to be threatened by someone with the strength and incentive to follow through. Leave this place. Leave this mermaid. And if I hear of anything bad happening to her—*ever and by anyone*—I will hunt you down and make you an exception to Sharkanian preference by eating you alive. Slowly. I'll let each bite heal before I take the next. And I'll start with your face."

I gnashed my teeth a scale away from his temple, ridiculously pleased when he cried out. Then, I released his hair and flicked my tail to give him enough space to swim away. He did, struggling to catch up to his friends who had already left him behind. When he was at the tip of the culvert and erroneously assumed he was a safe distance from me, he shot back in a quavering voice. "Prince Eric will hear about this!"

"Go ahead. Tell Prince Eric how you ganged up on a fellow Atlantian to accost her, but I thwarted you." I yelled after him. "I'm sure Princess Ariel would also like to hear your story."

Not sure why I mentioned Princess Ariel. Her words about *fish tales* from earlier tumbled in my head. These three mers would definitely tell a whopper. Would Prince Eric care to hear my side of the story? Would he seek out the mermaid to corroborate it all? Would she be brave enough to tell the truth to exonerate this ruthless, cold-blooded killer of a Sharkanian?

This could very well be exactly the excuse Atlantia needed to go to war with us. Or worse, exile us entirely. But I couldn't regret my choices or my actions, because the mermaid had needed my help and—

Oof! A body slammed into mine, arms clutching me and soft tendrils of hair caressing my face.

"Thank you thank you thank you!" The mermaid's muffled voice reached my ears from where she spoke against my neck, murmuring a steady stream of gratitude. She clung to me as firmly as a mussel and I was at a loss for what to do. Sharkanians didn't hug like this. We rarely touched, as we were a temperamental race that could easily misconstrue it as an act of aggression. Only close friends touched on occasion. But never like this. Even the act of fucking involved only the most necessary of touches: biting for both grip and clasper insertion.

I'd never before wanted a touch—a gentle touch. I'd certainly never wanted to return one.

Until now.

Her body was flush against mine, and her warmth and proximity was... doing things to me. I dipped my head just enough to inhale her natural scent, seagrass with hints of sugar kelp. It was a balm to my agitation and confusion, calming me while at the same time arousing me and making me want more. If I lowered my head a fraction further, I could put my lips on her skin. Taste her like I wanted. Her lithe body pressed to mine, rubbing against the two cartilaginous claspers on the front of my tail between us. The sensation shot heat through me as well as a growing desire to insert one of them.

The need to mate increased as she continued to hold me. If I didn't disengage her body from mine, I'd succumb to the Sharkanian drive to breed, which, like feeding, didn't take consent or preference into consideration. But if I rutted her, I'd be guilty of exactly what I'd fought three mermen to prevent.

Surely I was better than that. Better than them.

Feeling weirdly awkward, I patted her back and gently lifted her arms from my body, careful to slide her flesh the safe direction along my dermal denticles so they didn't scrape her. Once she was untangled from me, I set her out of arms-reach to take my leave.

But before I could disengage, her hands grabbed mine in their warmth. "Thank you for coming to my rescue! I'm so lucky you were in the area and heard them. Thank you for being so willing to help. What can I do to repay you for your kindness?"

She smiled at me, her expression trusting and pleading, and her question inspired all kinds of mental images of what I'd like to ask of her.

What I'd like to take from her.

I shook my head, to stop my swelling desire as much as her unwarranted adulation. "It was... it was no big deal."

"Don't be silly, it was a very big deal." She laughed at me. "Sharkanians usually don't come to anyone's rescue."

I frowned at those words and growled at her. "You are correct. So keep that in mind when you go bragging to your friends."

Her smile dimmed like I'd eaten her friends. She shook her head, her next words so soft I barely heard them. "Don't worry. I won't."

Then she set her shoulders back and looked at me with all the bravery she'd shown when facing three threatening mermen. "Believe it or not, helping others doesn't come naturally to many Atlantians, either. Especially if they are different."

She wasn't wrong. On that matter, Sharkanians and Atlantians were very much the same. However, the latter pretended otherwise.

I liked this mermaid. Liked her sensibility and courage. She looked small and frail, yet she'd stood up to her potential attackers. And she'd stood up to me. However much I might admire her, though, we couldn't be friends. Our world didn't allow for any such friendship—or more. Not knowing what else to do, I patted her shoulder. "Just... be more careful in the future. You were lucky this time that I happened to be near. But you should probably go back home."

Her bravery flagged and the light in her eyes faltered. "Oh. I. Um, I don't have... You know, you're right. I should go home."

I frowned at the sudden turn of her mood, but she wasn't my concern. Any Atlantian would be better off among their own kind than alone in the Wastes like a Sharkanian. We were solitary apex predators, but most Atlantian species were meant to be in schools with their families and friends.

Nodding at her decision to go home, I reached down to pick up the tuna chunk I'd dropped in preparation for battle. As I brushed off some of the sandy soil that clung to it, a loud rumble vibrated through the water. My heart in my throat and my senses on alert, I whipped around to place the mermaid between the culvert wall and me, keeping her as safe as possible from the unknown danger. My gaze scanned the area for the threat. Had the mermen returned with backup? Was there a quake in the area? An Opi Sea Killer passing by?

I heard the rumble again, behind me this time. I turned to face the danger, but noticed the mermaid looking miserable, as if she was in pain, her arms wrapped around her torso. The unseen danger could wait; I needed to tend to her needs first.

With two fingers, I lifted her face to mine. Before I could say anything, the rumble happened again. Emanating from her. Her belly.

I laughed in relief that we weren't in danger, but sobered immediately at her dejected expression. "Hey, little guppy." I tried to make my voice as soft and gentle as I could. "When was the last time you ate anything?"

Without waiting for her answer, I handed her my chunk of tuna. She didn't take it, but tentatively leaned in and took a tiny nibble before pulling back to chew, making a satisfied sound as if I'd offered her a feast.

"I've seen anchovies take bigger bites." I frowned and shoved the tuna toward her so she had no choice but to clutch it to her chest lest it drop back to the ground. She tried to return it, but I shook my head again. "No, I'm full. This is all for you."

She looked at me like I could swim in air before she tore off a bigger mouthful, obviously starved for sustenance. She hadn't answered my question, but her reaction to the tuna told me what I needed to know: she hadn't eaten in days. Maybe longer. She didn't look ill or injured, and now that the mermen were gone, my spores detected no fear or tension or pain. So where was her school? Her family? Why was she alone in the Wastes, unprotected and without food?

And why should I care?

I was a heartless Sharkanian. My only concerns were for my

kind and my own life. Not necessarily in that order. I should leave this mermaid to enjoy her meal. To go about whatever her business was out here, which wasn't any of my concern. I hadn't sought her out, hadn't wanted or needed the responsibility of another's life. I'd only intervened out of sheer curiosity. And because I could. Because any excuse to humiliate or fight an Atlantian was a win for all of Sharkania.

That excuse and that opportunity hopefully halfway back to Atlantia by now, the mermaid was safe and I should take my leave.

But I did not. What if the mermen were still nearby, waiting for an opportunity to pounce? What if she couldn't find more food and starved to death, thus mocking my efforts to keep her alive?

"Thank you. For saving me and for sharing your food." She spoke around a mouthful of tuna, but her soft voice caressed along my lateral lines, sending shivers through me like nothing I'd ever experienced. Not the chill of the deepest waters. Not even the anticipation of battle. These shivers shot straight to more pleasant areas of my body.

Ok, truth; I was melting on the inside, my harsh Sharkanian upbringing ill-prepared for the effect of her gratitude. She acted like I was a hero, like I was special, when I knew I was anything but. Regardless, I wanted to do more things to make her look at me that way. I opened my mouth to say something—what, I wasn't sure—but the expression on her face stopped me. Complete adoration. Like I'd created all the water's inhabitants.

I waved my hand as if I could wave away her unwarranted adulation. As if it didn't affect me. "Listen, you don't... you don't have to keep thanking me. I wouldn't have done any of that if I didn't want to."

Her expression softened further, her smile dreamy and her eyes half-closed with something that might have been absolute trust.

Spume. All my training, all my years of being stalwart and composed, determined, focused, fierce… it all evaporated like shallow waters. Not only did she seem intent on admiring me, I already wanted more. Craved her smile and soft voice more than I craved acceptance from the Atlantians.

Maybe the craving would pass, but at the moment, the thought of parting ways pained me more than my shoulder. But what to say to get her to stay, when I *should* send her away?

She saved me the internal conflict by speaking again "Thank y—er, I mean, I appreciate the meal. I… I haven't eaten anything in a while." She waved the much smaller chunk of tuna still clasped in her hand. "Please forgive me for my poor manners."

"Poor manners?" What could she possibly think she'd done wrong, and why would she think that any of this required an apology to me?

"Yes, you know, shoving food in my mouth so I can't make conversation."

She wanted to make conversation with me? I inspired a lot of different feelings, but the desire to chat was never one of them. I'd once told Princess Ariel that conversation was an activity Sharkanians enjoyed as much as eating, which was a lie. We were more of an *actions-speak-louder-than-words* sort of species. Actually, more of a *why-use-words-when-three-rows-of-teeth-are-just-as-effective* sort of species.

The fact this petite mermaid could somehow set aside her fear and hatred of my kind to even consider having a conversation shot joy more potent than the charge of an electric eel skittering through my body. I even chuckled. "Do not apologize for feeding your hunger before letting some silly expectation of manners and conversation get in your way. I'm Sharkanian… we're known for a lot of things, but our table manners are not one of them."

A current drifted between us, sweeping her long, silvery white hair in front of her face. I reached out to pull it back and tuck it behind her ear, not that it would stay there, but I was loath to let it hide her lovely face even as I continued my thought. "I would rather you sacrifice manners than your body's needs."

"My body's needs?" Her voice was even softer than before, almost a whisper threaded with hope, and she nibbled on her lips.

More of those pleasant shivers raced through me. The look of anticipation in her eyes, the gentle smile she offered me… my body interpreted her sincerity as desire, and blood flowed to my claspers, thickening them, preparing them for insertion.

I cleared my throat and thought about non-mating things. The elderly tuna. The merteens. Prince Eric. All of Sharkania. The surge of blood eased enough I could focus on answering her question. "Yes, your body's need for food."

"Oh. Those needs." She sounded disappointed, although I didn't understand why. She wasn't Sharkanian; she wouldn't have a need for violence. I'd satisfied her immediate need for food and safety. And after being nearly accosted by three aggressive mermen, I doubted she wanted to fuck.

So what else was there?

"By the way, I'm, um… my name's Mako."

Well, that was an awkward transition, but her face lit up with recognition and elation. "I know!" Bits of tuna dropped from her mouth. Tiny crumbs, unlike the mangled chunks my fellow Sharkanians often let float from their maws. She covered her mouth but couldn't stop her excited words. "I mean, I didn't know your name until now. But you're the one who patrols the palace grounds—"

"I'm not patrolling. I'm just swimming." I pulled her hand away from her mouth. The sight of chewed food didn't bother me, but not seeing her lovely features did. "You make it sound like I'm there in an official capacity."

"You might not be there to keep the peace, but that's what happens anyway." Her fingers threaded mine where I still held her hand. "I've heard lots of mers talk about bad things that almost happened, but then you floated by and the criminals swam away."

"Bad things?" Maybe the warmth of her hand in mine made my brain stop working, but I couldn't imagine what kind of bad things my mere presence could possibly deter. That would require imagining Atlantian existence was rife with villains and ne'r-do-wells, which I couldn't. Neither could I imagine Prince Eric would allow that sort of behavior in his kingdom. "What kind of bad things are you talking about? Neglecting to say *please* and *thank you*? Answering *How are you today* with the *none of your business*?"

She giggled, then her expression grew somber and her voice dipped to a whisper. "Bad things like stealing. Killing. Hurting. Threatening." Her grip on my fingers tightened. "Assaulting."

Hurting. Threatening. Like the merteens had done to me earlier. Assaulting, like those three mers were going to do to her. My gut clenched and my teeth ached to sink into their soft flesh. Why, oh, why had I let them swim away after a simple thumping?

I cleared my throat and shook my head. "Okay, so maybe I scare everybody away… regular mers as well as the unsavory sorts. But once I'm gone, the incentive to behave goes away and I'm sure the bad things start up again. My presence doesn't deter, it simply postpones."

She shook her head before I'd even finished, a secretive smile on her lips. "Yes, it doesn't stop everyone permanently. But maybe with more Sharkanians like you patrolling—"

I laughed at that. Laughed from my gut like I hadn't in a long time. "You want *more* Sharkanians? You realize we're Atlantian enemies? And that other Sharkanians are just as likely to eat you as they are to swim past?"

Not really. Again, we preferred our meals already injured or dead. But our reputation said otherwise, and I honestly couldn't vouch for what my fellow Sharkanians might do out of sheer boredom or when drunk on power. My own brother got a twisted laugh out of terrorizing innocent Atlantians.

"I said more Sharkanians *like you.*" She fiddled with the last few bites of tuna. Her shoulders lifted in a shrug. "You know… the strong hero type."

Hero? I choked on that word so hard I nearly blew a gill. "Oh, my sweet little guppy. I am not a hero. I'm not—"

"You saved me from three mermen without being asked or coerced. You shared your food with me, too." Her demeanor straightened, and the conviction in her voice was potent. "You swim the palace grounds and never once have you tried to attack, threaten, or even physically intimidate anyone. There's even a rumor that you were willing to fight Prince Eric to keep Princess Ariel safe. Who does that unless they're a hero?"

By the end of her list of reasons why I should be considered some sort of hero, she'd dropped the last bite of tuna to place her warm palms on my chest, her fingers digging into my pectoral muscles as if to convince me of the truth of her words.

All it did was make my desire flare.

I slid my own hands along the dip of her waist, fighting the urge to pull her flush against my torso. She gazed at me as if I made the tides ebb and flow, and not only did that encourage me to kiss her until she melted against me, it made me wish I was even half as wonderful as she seemed to think.

But I didn't. And I wasn't. And even though Princess Ariel had suggested I was more hero than villain, I couldn't pretend it was true, and I certainly couldn't let this lovely mermaid continue to be so deceived. "By Sharkanian standards, all that makes me is stupid and weak, little guppy—"

"You're not stupid and weak!" She objected, her fingernails digging in harder. *Spume*, I loved how passionately she defended my honor. Her nails eased from my flesh a bit, and she worried her bottom lip again, her voice softening. "And I'm not a guppy. I'm a grown mer."

Yes, she certainly was a grown mer, with a lean body surrounded by flowing whisps of silver hair. Her proximity shot electrical pulses through my pores and all around my nerves like lightning dancing along the water's surface. All I wanted to do was push her against the culvert wall and see just how much of her body I could lick before she shoved me away. I fairly shook with the need to explore her in the most carnal way.

I had to get control of myself. I was better than the mindless rutting beast my body wanted me to be.

Clearing my throat, I changed the subject. "I know you're not a guppy. But I don't know your name. What should I call you?"

She pulled her hands from my pectorals, and I instantly mourned their absence. I might not be a mindless rutting beast, but I still wanted her touch. She worried her fingers together. "P-three-two-six-one."

Her name was what? "That's not a name, little gu—uh, little mer. That's a number."

She canted her head and looked at me as if I were the one not making any sense. "Mako, when you're born in a school as large as mine, as large as most schools, there aren't enough names to go around."

That made sense. As numerous as we Sharkanians were, we weren't nearly as plentiful as most breeds of fish and mers. "Okay. But surely your family or your close friends call you something else. Something shorter and more… unique to you."

She looked down, but not before I saw her expression crumple. She struggled to breathe for a moment, then whispered so softly I almost missed the words. "I. I don't have any friends or family. I was… kicked out of my school."

My heart sank to my dorsal fin. While I knew very little about other fish and mers, I knew getting kicked out was usually a death sentence. What could she have possibly done to earn that punishment? Even if all my Sharkanian brethren thought I was weak or worthless—even if I sold my kind out to Prince Eric—they wouldn't kick me out. They might challenge me to fight... every single one of them... but I would never be summarily ostracized.

My arms wrapped around her and pulled her close before I was even aware I'd moved. She laid her cheek against my shoulder, her face buried in the crook of my neck.

"I can't begin to imagine what you've endured, separated from your school." I murmured as I simply held her. Comforted her as best as I could, which wasn't much. Sharkanians did not comfort each other. And knowing how abrasive my skin was, this hug couldn't be pleasant for her. But my body, nature, and upbringing mattered very little at the moment, with this lonely mermaid willingly in my arms.

I cleared away the strange lump of emotion in my throat and continued. "I-I know we just met. But I would be happy to call you a... friend. If you want that. You and I can be a school of two, until you find a better offer or grow tired of me."

By the elders, what nonsense was I spewing? I hadn't given my words any thought; they'd just bubbled up from somewhere deep inside me. But... invite her to be my friend? To join with me for however long she wanted? That was... that was something mers did. Mers who were in love and wished to bind their lives together. Sharkanians didn't bind themselves to one another. They even didn't pair off except for the few minutes it took to fuck. My body trembled at the completely uncharacteristic words I'd spoken.

Maybe she'd see how irrational my offer was, and would sensibly decline.

Her fingers dug into the muscles of my back, where she clung to me. Then she lifted her face to mine, her expression luminous with joy. "Do you really mean that? I can stay with you?"

I should laugh and tell her it was a joke. But I couldn't. Instead, my fingers gripped her hips tighter, excitement and terror both thrumming in my veins. I gulped water through my gills, hating that my response was uncertain. "Y-yes. I would not have offered if I did not mean it."

Spume, did I really mean it? I did, but I shouldn't. I shouldn't want her to remain in my company. She shouldn't want to hang around me. Nothing good would come of this if we stayed together. She'd be rejected by Sharkanians, if they didn't make a meal of her first, and definitely snubbed by Atlanians. And if I spent any more time with her near me, touching me, her scent in my nose... I'd lose control. I'd fuck her, for sure. She—

She. P-something-something-something. I pushed her away from my body, careful she wasn't scraped against my denticles. Then crossed my arms over my chest to lend gravity to my next words. "Yes, you can stay with me. It's not a very exciting existence, but you are welcome to share it. However, we need a name for you that isn't a bunch of numbers." I scrubbed my fingers along my jawline. "Do you have a name you'd like me to call you?"

She worried her hands together and shrugged, her expression forlorn. "I've never given it any thought. I've always simply been P-three-two-six-one. No one talks to me anyway, so it's never been an issue."

My heart broke for her. This beautiful, gentle mermaid spoke as if no one had ever cared about her. Was this typical for mer-schools? Such was the case for Sharkanian babies, left upon birth to fend for ourselves. But at least I'd been given a name before my mother swam away.

Glancing over the delicate-yet-feisty mer before me, I once again noted the shimmery scales that matched her long strands of silver hair. The light reflected off it in iridescent colors, like the inside of an oyster shell. Her coloring was very much like a—

"Pearl." I blurted. "What if I called you Pearl?"

Her lips quivered. "You would really do that? Call me Pearl?"

Spume, I'd upset her. I stumbled over my words to make amends. "Only if you want me to. We can find another name you like better. Or we don't have to find you a name at all if you don't want. I'll call you P-uh-three-whatever-the-rest-was…"

My words died on my tongue as she flung her arms around my neck again, her words rushing forth against my neck. "Don't you dare. I love the name Pearl. Please call me that. Please call me Pearl."

"Okay." Joy bubbled in my heart from her excitement and I pulled back to flash her a smile so broad the ocean could hardly contain it. Her gaze dipped to my mouth, and I worried for a moment the sight of all my teeth would scare her away, but it didn't. She lifted her gaze to mine, her expression as filled with wonder as I felt. "It's a pleasure to meet you, Pearl."

She melted into me again, her face in my neck and her voice soft with sincerity. "It's a pleasure to meet you, too, Mako."

My brain knew enjoying her touch this much was dangerous, but my body didn't listen, wanting more of this physical contact and her voice and her nearness. My hands sought her waist, and our fronts brushed together, sending waves of fizzy warmth through my body. I clenched my jaw against the arousal building within me. Pearl might be unafraid to be close, but I couldn't assume her voluntary proximity was an invitation to kiss her.

"Mako? Mako, may I…" She paused and pulled back until her face was a plankton's width from mine. "Mako, I want…" Her lips close enough I could touch them with mine on a sigh. *Spume*, maybe she did want to kiss me. "I need…" Her dainty fingers were on my face, and I couldn't move if the entire Atlantian army descended upon us. Her voice the barest whisper. "Please…Open for me…" Her chest brushed mine, her nipples puckered and scraping deliciously, and I gasped at the intimacy.

Then she stuck her hand in my mouth!

I froze, terrified to move lest I cut her with a tooth's edge, dying to ask why she'd do something so reckless but horrified I'd injure her. She tugged at something, and my hands gripped her waist, desperate to stabilize her or myself or our bodies together... whatever would keep from accidentally slicing her with my teeth.

"Got it!" She pulled her hand away with that triumphant cry, and showed me the stringy hunk of meat that had been lodged between my back teeth for weeks. A bite of dead sturgeon, I had tried to pry it out, but my fingers were too blunt and thick, I couldn't see inside my own mouth, and I absolutely refused to ask anyone for help with it. Not an Atlantian, and especially not a fellow Sharkanian. Not even Glut. That would be more embarrassing that admitting I'd been attacked by a group of merteens and Princess Ariel had saved me.

So I'd learned to live with the food in my teeth, and had forgotten it was there, resigned to the dull ache in my jaw.

Yet Pearl had come to my aid without being asked. Rather like I'd come to hers. Except there had to be a difference between the two. I'd helped her because I'd been in the area, well-fed, and bored. And it had been a good excuse to beat up on Atlantians. And, because, well, she had smiled at me, an occurrence so rare I'd obviously been too shocked to think clearly.

But a hunk of sturgeon lodged in my teeth was neither a dire enough situation to prompt help, nor anything anyone would freely fix. Especially when that meant sticking precious fingers into the deadly mouth of a Sharkanian. Maybe she'd helped me because she... liked picking rotting flesh out of teeth?

"Um... thank you?" I wasn't certain how to respond or how I even felt about her actions. It seemed such a small thing, but yet I was stunned stupid by her bravery. And her bizarre willingness to get near my teeth.

Which included her bizarre willingness to get near me.

"I thought it might be bothering you. And I wanted to help." Her face flushed with embarrassment, but she held my gaze. "I can also make a bandage for your injured shoulder."

Huh. I'd forgotten about my shoulder. I shrugged off my shock and slanted her a quizzical look. "Okay. But you realize fish never voluntarily put their body parts in a Sharkanian's mouth. If you were still hungry, you could have said so rather than hunt for meat in my teeth."

"Are you... being funny?" She blinked at me. "I didn't think Sharkanians joked."

"You're right. We don't joke." A mouthful of daggers did not lend to any sort of humor except for darkest, so I should leave the jokes for the clown fish. "I was merely commenting on the proof of your bravery."

"I'm not brave." She let the stringy sturgeon scrap drift away and put her hands against my pectorals. I should remove her small hands from my chest and distance myself from her, but couldn't find the strength or the conviction to do it. Before I could deny her statement, she continued. "I'm just... in love with you."

My fingers dug into her hips reflexively. My heart raced as if chased by the front edge of a tsunami. "You what? How can you be in love with me? We've only just met."

"We've only just met, yes." She worried her bottom lip, but did not retract her declaration. "But I've watched you for years. Watched you swim the palace grounds as if you had every right to be there."

"I do." I frowned at her. She'd watched me for years, and I'd never known? I was at a distinct disadvantage where her declaration of awareness and love were concerned, and it didn't set well with me. This mermaid had watched me all these years without my knowledge. What kind of predator was I if I couldn't sense such a thing?

No, that wasn't what had me out of my depth. It was... it was the lost time that I *could* have already spent with Pearl, if only I'd noticed her watching me. Or if she'd made herself known. Maybe I wouldn't have been so lonely. Maybe she wouldn't have been kicked out of her school.

"*I* know you have every right to be in Atlantian waters." She smiled, and it was blinding as the orb above the water's surface was rumored to be. "I also know everyone hates that they can't scare you away or make you feel unwelcome. I've watched you ignore the temptation to eat older fish. I've watched you help an injured mer carry stones and make the excuse that you'd already eaten so she would feel safe with you. I've watched you stop children who were mercilessly teasing a flounder with little more than a look. I've watched you pick up a vendor's display that another fish knocked over, and no one ever thanked you because they didn't see you do it... I've watched you be a better Atlantian than many Atlantians, and it never seemed to bother you that your good deeds went unnoticed. But I noticed."

I was shaking my head before she finished. "Pearl, I'm not... You can't possibly... I've never..." What was I trying to even say? The palace grounds had always called to me. Lured me to my doom like the mythological creatures believed to live above water's surface who kill fish by suffocating them in the air. I'd often wondered if I tempted fate by swimming the palace waters. But I'd assumed that fate would be my demise... not finding a beautiful mermaid who wanted to be with me.

The truth washed over me and settled deep in my cartilage. All this time swimming the waters of our world, I'd assumed I merely sought sustenance and the entertainment of making Atlantians uncomfortable. I hadn't realized what I'd actually sought—what I'd searched the ocean over for—was companionship. Someone to see past my dagger-teeth and my denticles and my culture's harsh values, to the fish beneath. To the Sharkanian who wanted to temper our embattled instincts so we could be accepted by Atlantians, rather than always be set apart.

Someone who knew the bleak emptiness of exclusion, and could view both worlds from enough distance to set aside our differences and focus on what made us the same.

And here this someone was. Here she was, in my arms, declaring her love, and all I really knew was that I didn't want it to stop. I didn't want to let her go or say good-bye to her. She felt right... She felt like a home I'd always longed for.

My claspers hardened again. As much as I wanted this touch and this proximity to Pearl, I needed to throw an ice flow over my growing desire. She might claim she loved me, but that didn't mean she wanted—

"Mako?" Her soft voice was a gentle caress along my lateral line. "Will you kiss me?"

I gulped in water at her forward request. My body quivered —I don't know why—fighting to not give into my mindless desire. After several moments, I was able to nod, hooked by Pearl's sweetness, sunk by her boldness. I couldn't let go of her now if all of Sharkania demanded it. I couldn't stop it; I couldn't hide it.

I wanted to kiss this mer.

Careful not to hurt her, I brushed my lips against hers. Her arms slid down my chest and around my torso as if she was afraid I'd stop. In slow, sensual increments, I deepened our kiss but that dance quickly grew desperate. I swiped my tongue along the seam of her lips on a silent request, and she instantly opened up, allowing me to explore her small teeth, twining my tongue with hers, her flavor bursting in my mouth. Her tongue twirled around mine, grazing the broad sides of my jagged teeth, cautious but unafraid. She'd thrust her hand in my mouth earlier, and now she did the same with her tongue, and I wanted to worship her courage.

"Pearl, I need to taste you. All of you. I've wanted to since I first saw you standing up to those mers." The desperation in my voice would have been laughed at by a fellow Sharkanian. But I didn't care. I wanted her to know how much I desired her.

She trembled in my arms. "Yes, Mako. I want you, too. Please don't stop."

"You'll tell me if you don't like it?" I pressed my forehead to hers. "Promise you'll say something if you want me to stop. Say something or push me away; I won't force you."

Pearl palmed my cheeks with her dainty hands. "I can't imagine not loving anything you do to me. But, yes, Mako. I will say something if it isn't absolutely mind-blowing."

I choked a small laugh as I drifted lower. "Okay, but maybe lower your expectations a bit."

Her giggle morphed into a sigh as I kissed my way down the side of her neck. Hungry, open-mouthed kisses across her clavicle and down her sternum until I divided my attention between her two uncovered breasts. I licked the puckered little nipples and carefully sucked the flesh between my lips as she threaded her fingers through my hair and fisted the short strands. Then I drifted further down, kissing and licking a meandering path along her lean figure. My hands roamed the soft skin of her back, tickled the pulsing gills at her side, and squeezed the smooth scales of her tail.

When I finally reached the delicate pink petals of her sex, which had blossomed forth from the recesses of her sex in the wake of her burgeoning arousal, Pearl arched back on a needy moan. The move pushed her sweet anemone into my face, as if I needed further encouragement to plunder those frilly folds. Sharkanian sex was as brief as it was functional, the focus strictly on insemination. Atlantian sex was far more engaged. In my years swimming the palace grounds, I'd glimpsed plenty of mers having sex, and the unintentional peeks proved it could be a languorous, hedonistic experience ending in pleasure for both parties.

I wanted that with Pearl. I wanted that *for* Pearl. Wanted to worship her in the most primal way. Taking care not to catch my teeth on her sensitized folds, I flicked and dragged my tongue over them, moaning as her flavor trickled down my throat. She was the most delicious creature I'd ever tasted, and I was instantly addicted to her. I kissed and licked her, my arms banded around her tail to hold her steady as she writhed and moaned and fisted my hair. Then I wriggled my tongue past her silky fronds and down into her warm opening, loving how her channel clenched me. I thrust and retracted my tongue, like I wanted to do with my claspers, and her moans grew louder as she held my face close. As if anything could pull me away.

Then she cried out her release, more of her succulent juices flowing around my mouth and down my throat and I could happily live on that for the rest of my life.

But I wanted something more at the moment. I desperately needed to bury one of my engorged claspers in her warmth. With a flick of my tail, I whipped up to kiss her lips again. She was coming down from the crest of her climax, her eyes bright with satisfaction and her limbs limp. I wrapped my arms around her torso to hold her lax body against mine.

"Pearl, you taste so good, I could subsist on just your flavor alone." I murmured against her temple as she melted against me.

While my own body still throbbed with desire, I loved how replete she looked. Content. I'd done that. I had provided her such pleasure. Not sure I'd ever before caused such a luminous expression on anyone's face, and the knowledge filled my heart with something I couldn't name because I'd never felt it before.

Her hands had wandered to my waist, and she ran them up my back, rubbing the painful direction against my denticles. I grabbed her arms and pulled away quickly, heart in my throat. "Don't do that. You'll hurt yourself."

She blinked, her hazy, happy expression sharpening to alarm at my tone. "What do you mean? Why would I hurt myself?"

"The dermal denticles of my skin. They're sharp when rubbed the wrong way." I palmed her hands and examined them for scratches. Fortunately, yet oddly, I saw nothing. "A merteen shredded his hand on my shoulder recently. While I have no regrets because he was a nasty parasite, I would hate for your soft skin to be scratched."

"Your denticles don't hurt me." Pearl's voice was soft and low, desire thrumming through its tenor, triggering my electroreceptor pores. Her hands slipped from mine and fingers traced up the ridges of my abdomen. My muscles flinched at the strange-pleasant sensation as well as the instinctive fear she'd be scraped. Her touch was light, yet firm enough to slice herself like the merteen.

Instead, she giggled as she showed me her fingertips, unscathed by my denticles. "It tickles, that's all. In fact..." She hugged me again, rubbing her nipples against my chest and moaning softly with pleasure at the contact. I froze, stuck between panic for Pearl's safety and utter rapture that she not only *wasn't* harmed, but obviously enjoyed the contact with my skin. I loved her caresses; was it truly possible to have more?

"This feels so good. *You* feel so good." Her voice was low and throaty.

Her hand reached between our bodies and stroked one of my claspers. I moaned into her mouth as she kissed me. Acting instinctively in the haze of my churning desire, I aligned my clasper at her opening, eager to push inside and claim her. I palmed and squeezed the succulent swells of her backside to hold her steady for my penetration, my muscles trembling with need and the effort to restrain myself.

Fortunately, some part of me could still reason, and I held back long enough to grit out desperate words. "Pearl, please tell me to stop now, because I'm going to fu- uh, make love to you rather, um, energetically."

She shook her head. "Mako, I promised to tell you if

something hurts. And I trust you to keep me safe. So please...
don't stop."

With that plea, I entered her tight heat through a series of
slow, careful thrusts, my clasper invading and her walls gripping
me so I struggled not to release immediately. Once fully buried
inside her, I took a moment to enjoy the sensation and the
expression of bliss on her face.

She looked like I felt. But the instinctive Sharkanian urge to
fuck her washed over me like a tidal wave. My voice was rough
with need as I gulped in water. "Pearl, I want you so much, I'm
not sure I can be gentle."

"I want you too much to want you to be gentle, Mako." She
banded her arms around my neck, her smile all the invitation I
needed. "Besides, you already promised me to fuck me
energetically."

Yes, I had.

So I thrust. Hard and fast, my fingers gripping her hips, my
engorged clasper bottoming deep inside her, my denticles
rubbing against her still-swollen folds. Pearl clutched me, our
chests sliding together, little mews and moans and gasps
escaping her throat with each thrust. The sand beneath us
churned from the force of my strokes, surrounding us in a
billowing cover from anyone who might pass us out here in the
Wastes.

My face pressed hard against Pearl's shoulder as I fucked
her, my teeth itching. Sharkanian sex was rough, violent,
involving biting the female to secure her submission. But Pearl
had already willingly submitted to me, and my hands kept her in
place so each snap of my hips didn't dislodge us from our vital
connection. I didn't need to bite her, and the thought of my teeth
tearing through her flesh was almost enough to make me push
her off my clasper for her own safety. Yes, her fingers could
withstand brushing against my skin, but even female
Sharkanians were irreparably scarred during sex.

Pearl's moans rose in volume and urgency. "Mako, don't stop. I'm going to come." Her arms banded my head and held me tight against her shoulder. "I just need... I need... Something more."

She thrashed in my hands, her tail twisting, her back arching, her hips rocking. I nearly lost my grip on her as she cried out. "Mako, bite me. Please."

I tried to shake my head, but she held me firm. I didn't dare fulfill her request for a bite, but I needed her to climax soon. My own release quickly approached, and I wanted her to ride that swell with me. As cautiously as possible, a challenge given how emphatically I fucked her, I pulled my lips back enough to nibble at her shoulder. The barest pressure from the tiniest point of my teeth, and she moaned louder.

"More! Please! Hard!"

Spume, she was going to make me come. I readjusted my mouth to the fleshiest part of her shoulder where it sloped gracefully toward her neck and bit down a little harder. She begged me for more, so I increased pressure until I felt my teeth sink into her skin. My heart skidded to a stop, but Pearl cried out her release, her body shuddering and her hands fisting my hair.

Her pleasure was such a beautiful creature, my own burst forth. I slammed my hips to hers one last time and held there, lost in euphoria and roaring out my release, loving this intimate connection and yet hating it was over.

We held each other for who-knew how long. Minutes. Hours. Until our heartbeats calmed and my body retracted from hers. Time held no power over us as we simply floated together,

"That was... that was amazing." I finally spoke, my voice hoarse. I had no idea what to say, and I knew my words weren't right. But they were honest. And if Pearl had watched me for as long as she claimed, she'd understand how awkward I might be in this situation. This post-coital bliss that had me wanting nothing more than to forever be in her embrace.

"It was more than amazing." Her voice was soft with wonder. "It was everything I'd hoped it would be, and more than I could have imagined."

I lightly traced a finger over the teeth marks on her shoulder. They were shallow enough not to draw any blood, but deep enough to mark her for life. She'd wanted my bite, and had climaxed from it, but that didn't keep regret from seeping into this languid aftermath. "I'm sorry I marred your beautiful body. These will leave a scar."

"And I will wear them with pride." She palmed my cheeks and met my gaze with sincerity. "In fact, I'd love more. Mark my entire body like that."

I shook my head but she spoke before I could. "It's what I've always wanted, Mako. Ever since I first saw you swimming the palace grounds, I wanted you. Wanted all of this with you and more." She worried her lip for a moment and her voice dipped to a whisper. "It's why I was kicked out of my school. Because I didn't want to reproduce with any of those mers. I only ever wanted you."

She stiffened on a thought and braced her hands against my chest as if she considered pushing away from me to escape. "I-I don't say that to make you feel... obligated to anything. I don't expect you to say anything back to me and it's probably the orgasm talking anyway, so you can ignore what I just said—"

I put a finger over her lips to hush her embarrassed babbling. My sweet little mermaid. My shimmery Pearl. She'd known for so long what I was only just discovering, and yet she'd given me permission to pretend our recent intimacy was meaningless and swim away from her. As if I could. As if I wanted to.

She'd have to try harder than that to get rid of me.

"Pearl, you're all I've ever wanted, but thought I'd never have." I kissed her deep and long, the truth of my words running strong and sure through my veins and her moans of pleasure humming in my heart.

"Um, Mako." She pulled away after long moments, a questioning look in her eyes. "Why are you still hard."

Her hand brushed my other clasper, still engorged and ready for penetration, and I moaned from the brief touch. "Because I have two claspers, and only used one. Don't worry, it will eventually soften."

"So, you mean we can do this again? Right now? We can make love a second time?" When I nodded, a sultry smile spread across her face. "Then what are we waiting for?"

Unable to deny Pearl much of anything, I returned her smile as I slid in my second clasper. We moaned as one and I set a leisurely pace, which gently carried our entwined bodies up and out of the culvert and into the open waters of the wastes. Whatever the future would bring us, I wouldn't stop now. I couldn't hide how I wanted to love this mer.

"Mmm Mako, you were right, this is delicious." Pearl exclaimed around a mouthful of tentacle from the partial squid I'd scavenged. For her, I would have hunted and killed something to eat, but she seemed perfectly happy with the foraging typical of my kind.

We'd wandered aimlessly for days, doing nothing but swimming, eating, talking, and fucking. To my surprise, simply being with Pearl was as satisfying as the physical connection. Being with her made me smile and laugh more than I'd known was possible for a Sharkanian General. And being with me made her feel safe. I hadn't believed her when she'd first confessed that; what fish in its right mind sought refuge *with* my kind instead of *from* us? Apparently, my Pearl did. And I loved her for it.

I loved her, period.

"Haven't seen you in a while, Mako." A familiar voice brought me up short, and I instinctively shoved Pearl behind me, my muscles ready for battle. I knew we'd swum back into palace waters based on the increased mass of lifeforms around us, as well as the expected stares. Atlantians shocked by the presence of a Sharkanian. Or shocked I swam hand-in-hand with one of their own. Maybe shocked she was with me willingly. Or possibly even shocked because I was smiling.

What I hadn't expected was a greeting committee of Prince Eric, Princess Ariel, and a few dignitaries who hung back and watched me with wary eyes. Prince Eric waved his hand toward me and continued talking as if I wasn't unwelcome. "I was afraid your absence meant something dire had happened to you. I'm glad to see you're well."

Tension thrummed in my veins. I had a combative history with Prince Eric, not the least of which was from trying to lure Princess Ariel away from him. In my defense, I hadn't known the depth of their feelings for each other at the time. Yet, he spoke to me just now like we were old friends.

Had Prince Eric been hit on the head with a block of basalt?

Before I could respond, Princess Ariel spoke up. "Mako, who is this beautiful mermaid you're hiding behind you?"

I hesitated, unwilling to expose Pearl to scrutiny. And maybe unwilling to share her, since I'd grown accustomed to her full attention these past several days. She squeezed my hand as if to reassure me, then drifted to my side and bowed to Prince Eric and Princess Ariel. "Thank you for the compliment, Princess Ariel. But I'm not nearly as beautiful as you."

My teeth gnashed at that, and I turned to Pearl to disabuse her of that opinion. "That's not at all true. You're as beautiful as any of the mers in Atlantia. You're the most beautiful, the bravest, the kindest, the—"

Laughter interrupted my tirade. Prince Eric laughed so hard, he bent at the waist and held a hand over his stomach. At least Princess Ariel had the courtesy to restrain her own laughter by biting her lips. But what was so funny?

After a moment, Prince Eric gathered his composure somewhat and shook his head. "Oh, Mako. You got it bad."

"Got what bad?" I frowned. He made no sense, and I tugged Pearl against my side protectively. If I had something bad, would they try to take her away to keep her safe?

Prince Eric gave me a look that was a confusing combination of understanding, approval, and perhaps a little sympathy. "You two look at each other like Ariel and I do. It's obvious you're in love, Mako."

"Yes I am. So what?"

Spume, that was not how I'd intended to confess my feelings to Pearl. I glance at her, worried she'd be mad. Of course, because she was amazing, she merely looked up at me with her luminous smile and love shining in her eyes.

Then Prince Eric had to interrupt the moment by speaking. "And I'm happy for both of you."

"I'm pleased to meet you, Pearl." Princess Ariel grabbed Pearl's free hand between her own and shook it up and down in some sort of bizarre greeting. "And I'm so happy Mako has you in his life, now. You are obviously a positive influence on him."

Pearl laid her head against my shoulder. The one she'd bandaged and was now nearly healed. Because she was perfect. "Mako is wonderful, and I'm very happy to be with him."

I kissed her temple, ready to end this conversation and find a quiet place so I could properly declare my feelings to her and then hopefully make love to her again. But Prince Eric cleared his throat and spoke again. "Mako, I'm glad you're here; I have an offer for you."

That pulled my attention away from my escape plans. "An offer?"

"Yes. There have been rumors that you often swim the palace grounds, helping fish, *not* eating anyone, and acting as a crime deterrent by your mere presence."

"Guess I'm not the only one who noticed your good deeds." Pearl squeezed my arm.

"No, you're not, Pearl. Many mers have noticed and reported to us." Princess Ariel confirmed. "Mako, as a Sharkanian, you command a healthy amount of respect. And your actions have earned you a lot of admiration."

Prince Eric held his hand out to me. "Because of this, I'd like to offer you the official position of Officer of the Law."

Why the bizarre greeting? He already knew me. I stared at his hand, only able to respond with the truth. "But I already have an official position. I'm a Sharkanian General."

"Yes, you are. But I'm hoping you can be both." Prince Eric kept his hand out. "Ariel and I have talked at length about how to break down the barriers between Sharkania and Atlantia. Build bridges instead."

"Bridges?"

"Yeah, you know, structures that carry roads across bodies of water to— um, never mind. Bad word choice. Let me rephrase: We want to alleviate the tension between our peoples while strengthening better relations. I can't force co-existence and acceptance; that's a recipe for disaster. But if we maximize each other's strengths—if we slowly integrate Sharkanians into positions that give them the best chance for success—it will ultimately benefit everyone."

That was a lot of words, many of which swam over my head. But I understood Prince Eric wanted what I wanted: for Sharkanians and Atlantians to get along. To end the fear and hate and mistrust that permeated our societies.

But did our societies want that?

"You can still continue your duties as a General." Prince Eric continued, his hand still out there. "We'll make a schedule that works for you. And hopefully, you can recommend other Sharkanians who would be a good fit for the position to help fill any gaps of coverage."

I immediately thought of Glut, but managed not to blurt out my brother's name. Honestly, I wasn't certain he'd accept the job. Instead, I blurted a question. "Why are you doing this now? You've been in charge for years."

Spume, I didn't mean to sound quite so antagonistic.

Prince Eric finally moved the hand to rake it through his hair on a self-conscious chuckle. "Well, to be honest, I haven't always been a merman. I'm from another world, but was somehow transported here, like Ariel. So, I wasted a lot of those previous years just trying to get back to my own homeworld. When I finally gave up, I had to acclimate to the Atlantian society, including my role as Prince. And I assumed the bias against Sharkanians had been rightfully earned. Until Ariel reminded me there are always two sides to a story. She encouraged me to seek better understanding, and it's led me to realize that just because these hostile feelings between our kind are grounded in an embattled history... we don't have to perpetuate it."

Ariel slid her arm around Prince Eric's waist, gazing at him the way Pearl gazed at me, before she turned to smile at me. "Those are really big words to say we want peace. We want to make a better future for all of us, Atlantian and Sharkanian alike, and this is the first of many steps toward that goal. You would be an ambassador helping to link our worlds."

Could I be both a Sharkanian General and an Atlantian officer? Would my people allow it? Could they stop me? And was I up to the pressure of being an Officer of the Law? More importantly, was I up to the responsibility of being an ambassador of peace?

I turned to Pearl, hoping she would give me some guidance. Prince Eric obviously welcomed Princess Ariel's insight, so it couldn't be a sign of weakness that I wanted Pearl's opinion on this matter. I brushed her hair from her face and palmed her cheek. "What do you want me to do?"

She traced her fingertips up my abdomen, as had become her habit. My muscles jumped at her touch. "I want you to follow your heart, Mako. Follow your heart and I will follow you."

Follow my heart. Pearl was my heart. And she gazed at me with complete trust. Trust that I would keep her safe and provide for her. How could I do that if I was busy being a peace ambassador? Guess I would have to trust Prince Eric. Trust that this wasn't a trap. Trust that he truly wanted the kind of future I had long hoped for. If so, I'd have the power of Prince Eric behind me to safeguard Pearl. My standing as a Sharkanian General would do the same. I had been willing to hunt and kill just to feed her, was I willing to accept this offer for her as well?

With all my heart. Well, with all my heart not already occupied with loving Pearl.

I brushed my lips across hers, pulling her close, then turned to Prince Eric and Princess Ariel. "I accept your offer. I want to give Pearl a safe and happy life. I want to help broker peace between our people."

Prince Eric smiled and stuck his hand out, but Princess Ariel threw herself into my arms with an excited squeal before I could take it. "I'm so happy you said yes!" She pulled back, her expression nearly as luminous as Pearl's.

Laughing, Prince Eric carefully untangled her arms and pulled her into his, apparently undisturbed by the fact she'd hugged another male. With Princess Ariel lovingly tucked against his side, he stuck his hand toward me again. This time, I didn't hesitate. I grasped his hand in mine and we shook, the motion signifying a bond of sorts. A promise that we were in this together.

With Pearl at my side, loving me without expectation or condition, and Prince Eric and Princess Ariel before me, pledging their commitment to work toward peace, some elixir of weird emotions welled up inside me. It was hope. And purpose. And acceptance.

And love.

"Come on, we'll show you the palace room you can live in when you're in Atlantia." Princess Ariel waved us forward. Pearl and I followed, her warmth against my side. "Then we'll give you some privacy so you can… well… makes yourselves comfortable."

"We'll be living in the palace?" Pearl's voice was filled with wonder.

"Living and *other activities*." I chuckled as I reached around to swipe a fingertip along the slit hiding her sex. Funny how so much of my life as a Sharkanian had been spent keeping up the appearance of strength, always afraid someone would find a weak spot in those scales. But I wasn't afraid of looking weak with Pearl, because I was stronger with her at my side. "I love you, Pearl. Let's make this world the best it can possibly be. Together."

~

POOR UNFORTUNATE SOULS

Ursule has an uncanny knack for problem-solving which has earned him the grim moniker Sea Witch. Unfortunately, it doesn't prevent pesky merpeople from approaching him with their problems. Until two captivating eel-maids invade his lair, wishing for nothing more than his company. And his talented tentacles.

"Excuse me, Mr. Sea Witch."

A quiet voice behind me preceded a light tug on one of my tentacles. The interruption to my hunt for dinner was irritating enough. But for some random mer to have the audacity to touch me… well, it practically sent me into a rage.

Which wasn't saying much. Most interactions with mers tipped my already-grumbly nature into downright irate.

Instead of attacking—because I'd been focused on finding dinner, not on how many mers might be at my back—I whirled around, belling out my eight tentacles and the webbing between them to appear as large and intimidating as possible. The muscles of my skin tensed for a prickly texture and turned me a warning shade of bright yellow. Added to my surly reputation, the whole effect was often enough to scare away even the most determined opponent.

In hindsight, my response might have been a bit excessive. Especially as the lone little mermaid who'd sought my attention flinched and paled in fear, a faint yelp escaping her lips before her eyes rolled back and she looked moments from fainting and sinking to the sea floor.

I deflated and my skin returned to its normal black color. "Next time, don't touch me."

Yes, my voice was hard and unyielding. No, I didn't care. I had a knack for figuring things out, and I'd long ago figured out that being nice to any mer-folk only fostered in them the belief they had a right to my time and talent. Even when my attitude was as spiny as a sea urchin, they sought me out to help solve their problems.

As if I could fix everything.

No, I can't make you pretty. Or thin. Or rich. Or make Prince Eric fall in love with you—thank the Tides he'd finally found his one true love and she was wildly popular with the mers, so I never had to hear *that* particular request again. I was smarter than the average mer... but I wasn't a miracle worker.

Still, they seemed determined to believe I was.

Like this frail little thing, who had recovered enough to shake her head and lift an imploring gaze to mine. "I'm so very sorry, Mr. Sea Witch." Her voice quavered with a strange combination of remorse and hope. "I'd called your name a few times already and you didn't hear me. I didn't mean to touch you. I was just desperate for your help."

I crossed my arms over my chest and glared at her. Oh, I'd

heard her. I'd simply ignored her. "No, you didn't call my name. *Sea Witch* is my designation. Ursule is my name."

Before she could jump to any unwelcome conclusion, I clarified my statement. "Don't call me by my name."

Duly deflated, the mermaid breathed in a gill-full of courage and addressed me again. "I understand. I merely wanted to ask for your help in securing the affections of a merman I've secretly admired for as long as I can remember."

See? Everyone thought I was a miracle worker. And by the determined set of her chin, I could tell she wouldn't take *no* for an answer. My tentacles worked independently enough to continue dipping into tiny nooks and crannies of the coral reef next to us, searching for small fish or crustaceans to eat while I disabused this mer of her belief I could help her. "Listen, I have no powers over the heart. If you've been pining over this mer all that time and he hasn't returned the sentiment yet, there isn't anything I can do to make him fall in love with you."

I'd have to understand the emotion first. But I'd never known love. For all our tentacles, we cecaelias weren't touchy-huggy creatures. In fact, we kept to ourselves, with the brief exception of procreation. But even that was about as romantic as taking a piss. All I knew about the emotion of love was what I'd witnessed from others who'd claimed to experience it. Meaning, I knew love made creatures do stupid things. Like seek out the assistance of Atlantia's legendary Sea Witch.

So, help a mer find the love of her life? Not high on my fun list.

Tongue-kissing a Sharkanian ranked higher, and I was way too intelligent to attempt that painful maiming.

Yet this little mer was already shaking her head as if she didn't believe me. As if there were abundant rumors to the contrary. Proof that I'd played successful matchmaker to hundreds of mer couples.

Pffft. As if.

"I don't expect you to make him fall I love with me." Her voice was practically a whisper, like she was afraid someone might overhear our conversation and ridicule her for it. "I just want him to notice me. And I thought that maybe if you pretended to attack me when he was around. He would see it and try to save me. He's very shy, but he's also very brave."

She flashed a hopeful smile at me, and lifted a sack filled with something that smelled tasty. "And I can pay. I have fresh scallops for you."

Curse the Tides, how did she know those were my favorite? Before I could again decline her request for help, my tentacles had snatched the bag from her hands and curled around its precious contents. Having independent limbs was a blessing and a curse. I forced them to return to bag to the mermaid. "You want me to attack you—"

"Just pretend to."

"Not the point. You want to give this mer the impression I am attacking you—when I've never been violent with anyone—so he can rescue you. From me. Which means I'm going to get touched. Possibly hit. Maybe even injured."

I shook my head. "I'm not in the habit of making myself look weak or abusive, even if it's pretend. That's not a reputation I care to cultivate. Perhaps you should ask Mako the Sharkanian. I hear he was recently appointed Officer of the Law in Atlantia. He might have better ideas on how to impress this mer if violence is your answer."

The devastation on her face almost melted my three hearts. Well, maybe one of them. I might not want a reputation as a bully who was easily beat, but I *did* have a reputation for solving things. I sighed, water passing quickly over my gills. I guess could help her. If only to earn the payment of scallops.

I forced the next words past my lips. "But if I may suggest a different way to gain this merman's attention, I can mix up a lotion that will smell so irresistible, he won't be able to help but notice you."

Hope glistened in her eyes. "You'd really do that? For me?"

No, but I'd do it for the scallop payment. Fortunately, I managed not to roll my eyes and forced a nonchalant shrug. "It's what I do. It's what I live for."

The mermaid squealed in a level of delight contrasting the dry lie I told. She shot toward me as if to throw her arms around me in a—*shudder*—hug. I tensed to shove her away, but she caught herself at the last moment, and pushed the bag of scallops against my chest instead.

"You're the best." Her voice was still quiet, but threaded with so much exuberant joy that even my own withered hearts beat a little lighter. Which was a bizarre sensation. Perhaps I was dying. Perhaps I had indigestion from my morning meal of prawns. I clutched the bag and prayed to the Tides my condition was the latter. The mermaid glanced up at me through shuttered eyelids and traced her fingertips down my abdomen. "So, should I come to your den to get the lotion?"

My tentacles curled as a fissure of fear shot through my body. Not from the sultry tone of her voice, the evident fact she was trying to seduce me while supposedly wanting another, or even her unwelcome touch. It was the thought of having her in my den. That was my personal space, my home, my sanctuary. The place where I sought refuge from the teeming mass of life inhabiting Atlantian waters. I would never willingly invite someone to join me there.

Not even for procreation.

Atlantians never expected privacy while they fucked. Most of them lived out in the open waters anyway, so all aspects of their lives occurred with an audience.

No matter, I still wasn't inviting this mermaid to my den. I pulled away from her touch and two tentacles lifted to deter any additional approach. "Absolutely not. I will find you in a few days with the lotion. If the merman doesn't fall for you, he is a complete fool and you should find someone else worthy to pin your affections on. Regardless, I will not help you again."

With a powerful flick of my tentacles and an expulsion of water through the gills at my side, I jetted away from the mermaid lest she try to touch me again. Or suggest I could be next in line if a relationship with the merman didn't work out. It had been a while since I'd fucked anyone, but an orgasm wasn't worth the emotional baggage she no doubt brought.

And honestly, I didn't want to be anyone's second choice.

Ew. Just… *Ew*.

Whipping around a bend in the coral so I was no longer in her line of vision, I abandoned my hasty retreat and slowed to a crawl. My tentacles walked and pulled me across the craggy terrain of the reef with the maximum blend of efficiency and velocity. I was built for dexterity, not speed. Certainly not sustained speed. Short bursts of escape I could handle, but they were exhausting.

And exhausted was a dangerous state for a cecaelia. I might be smarter than the average mer, which meant I was smart enough to acknowledge I wasn't top of the food chain. Unlike a Sharkanian with their thousands of teeth and tough, rough skin that acted as both protection and weapon, most of my limbs were squishy and tender. And I probably tasted delicious, like the scallops I hugged to my chest. Unlike the scallops, I didn't have the protection of a crunchy shell.

Hmmm, maybe I could craft my own protective defense with the shells of my dinner. I could be nearly as unstoppable as a Sharkanian if I clothed myself in a scallop shell to pair with my big brain.

No, bad idea. A scallop shell suit wouldn't allow for the flexibility my tentacles enjoyed. I had the advantage of being able to stretch and squish and fit into almost any space; a suit of shells would instantly negate that. Plus, everyone would hear my approach as the shells clanked against one another. I'd never find any dinner without the stealth my mobile tentacles currently allowed me. So, yes, a shell suit would protect me, but I'd starve as a result. And carrying its added weight would exhaust me more than even a swift retreat.

And have you seen their shells? I would constantly pinch my tender tentacles with those sharp corners and edges. Guess I couldn't have my scallops and my scallop suit, too.

"Ursule, I'm so pleased you could join us."

A familiar voice pulled me from my musings, and I glanced around. Curse the Tides, I'd managed to wander into a large assembly of mers and other Atlantian citizens while I'd been deep in thought. My big brain was going to be the death of me. Or, at least, a serious inconvenience. The crowd of Atlantians had parted to allow me in their midst, their shocked, awed whispers finally reaching my ears now that I wasn't so distracted.

It's Ursule, the Sea Witch.

He once saved my sister from a Sharkanian.

I knew a mer who refused to trade with the Sea Witch, and the next day she choked on a prawn and died.

Do you think he could make me thinner?

Forcing my attention away from their misdirected mutterings, I faced the mer who'd addressed me. He hovered in the middle of the gathering, patiently waiting for me to respond. Prince Eric. We certainly weren't good enough acquaintances for him to call me by my name, but who was I to correct the beloved Prince Eric, ruler of all Atlantia?

Eric wasn't even a real prince. Not like Atlantia's former royalty. Before I was hatched, the real king had been supposedly killed during a skirmish with the Sharkanians—although my distrusting gut told me there was more to that story —and he'd had no offspring or successors. Then, several seasons ago, Eric had shown up as if by magic, looking unlike

113

the typical mer. His face was rounder, his eyes set in front rather than toward the sides, and his lips thicker. The flesh of his torso was a pinker tone than the typical greenish-gray mer, which contrasted nicely with the dark blue and silver-gray of his fin.

In spite of his non-traditional appearance and whatever tide brought him to Atlantia, Eric was skilled at managing his many responsibilities. I did not envy his position in the least. Having to balance the immediate desires of individual Atlantian citizens and the long-term needs of the whole community, he was constantly bombarded by demands. The thought of which twisted my gut because I would *haaaaate* that much interaction with Atlantian citizens. They bothered me enough as it was, and I wasn't in any position of leadership like Eric.

I'd never admit it out loud, but a small part of me admired Eric for willingly taking the helm of Atlantia's kingdom and ensuring our world continued to thrive. I definitely was grateful he'd arrived before the ambassadors tried to slate me in that position.

I dipped my head just enough to be respectful. "Your Highness, I wasn't aware there was a party. I am more than happy to leave if my presence is unwelcome."

"Nonsense, you are always welcome." Eric waved away my comment as if I were truly concerned my presence would be a hindrance. I'd have to craft better excuses to get out of future social situations such as this. "I'm introducing Princess Ariel to the reef area today. We haven't had much of a chance to travel this far from the palace to see the rest of Atlantia."

Curse the Tides, he was such a *nice* mer.

He turned to the mer beside him. She was lush and colorful, with a vibrant green tail and long hair pinker than a starfish. She had generous breasts hardly covered by the large scallop shells she wore. Although they didn't offer her any protection, she didn't have to worry about being pinched by the shells. Maybe that was the key to my scallop suit: make sure the shells were far enough apart—

"My love, this is Ursule, the famous Sea Witch I was telling you about." Eric's voice interrupted my musings again.

The mer he spoke to drifted closer to me, her lips upturned in a smile that revealed even rows of white teeth. She clasped the sides of her fin as if she wanted to reach for me, but was afraid.

"It's such a pleasure to meet you." Her voice was warm and welcoming. So, not afraid. Maybe just respectful? That would be a novel experience. "Eric has told me so much about you."

As if acting of its own volition, much like my tentacles, her hand shot toward me, fingers outstretched and palm to the side. I stared at her hand, not understanding what the stance meant and painfully aware of all the other mers watching this exchange. Surely someone as smart as me would know what to do in this situation, right? Was I the only who didn't intrinsically understand this social cue?

Before I panicked—while I hated the fact everyone assumed I could solve all their problems, I equally hated the possibility Atlantians would laugh at my slightest show of ineptitude—Prince Eric bridged the awkward space between Princess Ariel and me, murmuring just enough for the three of us to hear and no one else. "My love, Ursule isn't what you would call a touchy-feely sort of mer."

Princess Ariel's hand drifted back to her side in a forced casual manner and she nodded in understanding, her smile broadening. "I completely understand, and I apologize if I made you uncomfortable. Would you prefer I call you Ursule, or Mr. Sea Witch?"

I shrugged instinctively, as if I didn't care. Of course I cared. There was no one in Atlantia I wanted calling me Ursule. But if Princess Ariel was Eric's one true love—and by the besotted expression on his face as he gazed at her, she was—and the fact she'd so graciously retracted her hand, I should allow her to call me whatever she pleased. "Princess Ariel, you may refer to me however you wish."

Did my voice sound convincing enough? No, because she shook her head and laughed, drifting a tad closer but not so close I wanted to bolt.

"That doesn't answer my question." Her voice quieted so only the three of us could hear her next words. "What do *you* want me to call you? Ursule? Sea Witch? Doc Ock? Hank? Hey you? You tell me your preference, and I will abide."

My tentacles fidgeted nervously against the rocky sand. Hopefully no one noticed. I glanced at the crowd around us, wishing I could have this conversation without an audience. But, short of being rude—and I didn't dare behave so in front of the Atlantian ruler—there was no way to avoid responding. I drew a deep breath of water and siphoned it out. "Princess Ariel, in truth, I don't like anyone talking to me, regardless of what they call me. I prefer to be left alone."

A twinkle of humor glinted in her eyes. What had I said that was so funny?

She leaned forward and whispered so only I could hear her words. "I completely understand, *Left Alone*. Please don't ever feel obligated to talk to me, although I will always welcome it. Have a lovely rest of your day, *Left Alone*. And may the waters always be warm and the currents always at your back." She closed one eyelid in an exaggerated motion, then turned to Eric, her voice back to a normal volume. "Sweetie, could you please show me that outcropping over there?"

Eric held out his arm for her to take, then led her, and the sycophantic crowd of onlookers, away from me.

Had Princess Ariel just saved me from further social interaction?

And had she named me *Left Alone*?

Thinking back on my words, if she'd taken my comment in the most literal manner, that was exactly what I'd asked her to call me. *Left Alone*. A chuckle bubbled up my throat. That was a cunning move, and I understood why Eric would fall in love with her. Or at least admire and desire her to a point he was comfortable claiming the emotion as *love.*

Love was a conundrum I had yet to solve, even with all my skills. But rather than muddle through the possibilities, I focused on my trip to my den. I didn't dare get waylaid by a mer with a request or stumble upon another awkward meet-and-greet again.

Even with the slower pace of walking, I was soon at my den entrance. Situated in a shallow chasm distant enough from the coral beds swarming with potential food that I was afforded my precious privacy, it was still close enough that I could readily access my meals. As much as I'd love to never see another Atlantian, I did need to eat.

But a noise coming from inside my den made me pause. It sounded like… something crunching. And soft giggles.

Giggles?!

My skin clenched and my hearts hammered. Something was in my den. The exact situation I never wanted to happen had happened. I leaned in to hear better, clutching the entrance in case I needed yet another quick getaway and wishing I was built to be a fighter instead of a thinker. Sadly, my soft tentacles, as adroit as they were, weren't exactly battle-ready weapons. And my small cache of weapons was in my den. With the intruder.

Maybe I should find Mako and ask for a spear I could carry with me in one of my eight tentacles. Not that he could help me. He was Sharkanian; his weapons were his many teeth and his apex predator's swift reaction. I wasn't an apex predator, unless you were a small scallop or other tasty morsel. I was an apex thinker.

I was smart. A problem-solver. Perhaps I could approach this invasion of my home without having to get physical.

Creeping slowly along the den's dark, narrow entrance, I continued to listen for clues as to what I might find. More crunching and what sounded like chewing. What would be in my den a mer could crunch on—*Oooooh*. Thanks to my independent tentacles doing their own thing, I often brought home more food than I could eat. Rather than return it or throw it out, I kept it for another meal. Although what often resulted was small crabs infiltrating my lair to dine on my leftovers. I didn't mind. They ate the food I'd discarded, and I ate them when I didn't feel like foraging.

It was a win-win for me.

But other than the slight sound of skittering across my den floor, the crabs never made a noise. I certainly never heard them crunching. Or giggling. Which meant something else was in my den crunching on *them*. Crunching on my symbiotic food source. And then giggling about it.

"Flottie, you were so smart to explore this cave." A female voice reached my ear, light and lively and effervescent with joy. It tickled across my body like bubbles from a thermal vent, and I shivered, my tentacles wriggling in pleasure.

"Fortunately, whoever left it such a mess must not know these crabs moved in." Another female voice responded. That meant there were *two* intruders in my den. Two uninvited guests. And I should have been furious about the fact, except the low, silky timbre of the second voice cascaded down my body like fine sand. A stirring caress unlike any I'd ever known but suddenly wanted more than I wanted my scallops.

The two voices shot arousal down my spine and straight to my cock. I clenched my teeth against the rare burst of desire and ignored the insult to my homekeeping skills as I fought to control my physical reaction. My camouflage abilities activated, coloring me the dark gray of my den walls as I crept closer.

The smooth voice continued. "We should eat quickly, just in case the owner returns."

Unable to hide my curiosity any longer, I leaned forward to peer into my den. Two moray eel-maids lounged against the side of my bed platform, plucking skittering crabs from the floor and dining like queens.

I was stunned silent for a moment. Mer-eels were rarely seen in this area, a fact for which I was glad. They were cutthroat predators and cecaelias like me were often their prey. Would these two mer forego the crisp outer shell of those crabs for my soft, chewy tentacles?

And why was one particular tentacle anything but soft at the thought?

Few mer-folk were distinguishable from one another, in my opinion. But these two eel-maids were each notably unique in their own right. One was dark with light spots and far more curvaceous than an a mer should ever be, but my fingers itched to trace the rolling landscape of her figure. The other was light with dark spots. Slender and sleek and my tentacles quivered at the thought of exploring her streamlined length. Their long tails were intertwined like lovers, and I experienced a momentary pang of guilt for spying on this rather private moment, even if it occurred in my own den. Or maybe the pang was jealousy for an intimacy I'd never experienced.

No, I'd fucked enough over the years. This must be merely hunger pangs for the scallops in the bag I still clutched.

Both intruders paused, lifting their faces and sniffing at the water. Mer-eels had an excellent sense of smell and they no doubt smelled my bag of scallops. Had I known they were the cause of the crunching noises emanating from my den, I would have left my bag of scallops at the entrance. But then I'd have nothing to possibly distract them from my own scent.

"Do you smell that, Flottie?" The one with the slender figure, obviously the one called Jettie, leaned toward the other one.

Flottie hummed in sultry agreement, squeezing Jettie's tail in a manner that was more than merely friendly. "Scallops. And something else."

I wouldn't be able to fight them or swim away; they were far faster and stronger than me. My only choice lay in trying to make a good impression.

And by that, I meant appear as awe-inspiring as possible.

Flottie sniffed at the water again. "Something like—"

"Like the owner of this den." I growled as I dumped my camouflage and entered the den in a flourish of tentacles and belled webbing. My anger and sheer size were often enough to frighten away most mers.

Most.

These two eel-maids didn't even flinch. In fact, they sat where I'd found them and stared at me, their eyes large and unblinking. Not only were they not scared, they barely looked concerned. All the bravado I'd mustered left me to scamper across my den floor like the crabs scurrying for safety. Curse the Tides, these two eel-maids were going to devour me.

I was going to be their next meal.

"Flottie, did I eat a bad crab?" Jettie spoke softly, her eyes never leaving me and her body motionless, ready to attack. Actually... she looked less poised for action and more stunned into inaction. Stunned? That made no sense, but I couldn't ask because she continued talking. "Did I eat a bad crab and now I'm hallucinating? Please tell me I'm not just imagining that Ursule the Sea Witch is here in this den with us."

She recognized me?

Flottie licked her lips, and the slow swipe of her tongue across her mouth sent a tingle down my chest. My stomach muscles clenched and my tentacles trembled. I frowned at my body's bizarre reaction as she responded to Jettie, her eyes never glancing away from me. "You're not dreaming. We must have wandered into his den on accident."

"This wasn't an accident; this is a sign the Tides have blessed us!" Jettie squeed and bolted up, untangling her tail to drift closer to me. My frown deepened, but she seemed oblivious to the supposed threat of angering the Sea Witch. In fact, she clasped her hands against her chest and twirled as if with uncontained glee. "We've spent so many long days talking about how much we wanted to meet Ursule. To see him up close. To talk to him."

Was she still talking to Flottie? Or to herself? Or, maybe even me? Jettie hugged herself on a shiver. If she wasn't still smiling so broadly, I might have assumed she was nervous.

"The Tides have indeed answered our wishes." This was whispered like she was afraid I really was a figment of her imagination and would dissolve into nothing if she spoke too loudly or moved too eagerly.

I crossed my arms over my chest and glared at her. I knew exactly where this was going. There was only one reason anyone was ever glad to see me, so I waved away her excitement. "Yes, yes, the Tides are truly generous and brought you to me. What is it that you wish. And before you speak, keep in mind that I can't kill anyone, I can't make anyone fall in love with you, and I can't bring back anyone back from the dead."

Jettie merely cocked her head to the side and scrunched her face in confusion. Flottie unfurled from the floor and wrapped an arm around Jettie's waist in a stance that was combination protective and seductive. I felt the weight of her arm as if it rested against my own flesh, and I had to swallow down the rising need to know that kind of touch. I was Ursule the Sea Witch. A cecaelia. A loner. I didn't want anyone's touch, let alone any mer who'd entered my lair—unbidden and unwelcome —to ask for wish fulfillment.

Flottie rested her temple Jettie's for a comforting moment, then shook her head, her eyes never leaving me. "We didn't come here to ask you to fulfill any wishes. In fact, we didn't even know we were in a den that was presently inhabited. Much less in a den *you* had claimed as your own. Please forgive our intrusion. And for eating your crabs."

She waved her hand to indicate the den and it's now-scant

crustacean inhabitants. I didn't really care about the lack of crabs. More would no doubt come thanks to my messy homekeeping habits. But there were more pressing matters to address.

I shrugged away her excuses and got to the heart of it. "Why are you here?"

Flottie twined her fingers at her tiny waist, her expression honest and without any hint of anger or annoyance. Odd, because I usually offended the rare few mers who weren't trying to get something out of me. The many who were, looked past my irksome manners to ingratiate themselves. But I couldn't dwell on those facts because Lottie's move had pushed her lovely breasts—covered with a simple band of wide kelp rather than shells like Princess Ariel had worn—upward, and my eyes snagged on the motion. I never paid attention to a mer's body. Why consider the details of the body when the mouth always aggravated me with its idiotic requests?

But this body was particularly lovely, especially the tempting swell of her cleavage above the kelp band and her dark coloration which blended into that of her tail. I tracked the rise and fall of her chest with the ferocity of an Atlantian palace guard, until I realized she had yet to answer my question.

When my gaze lifted to hers, her lips lifted to one side in a smirk. I'd been ogling her body and she knew it. Not only that, but she was obviously in a meaningful relationship with Jettie. While neither seemed upset, embarrassment speared through me at my uncharacteristic behavior. I covered that with a more typical gruffness. "You haven't answered my question. Why are you here, if not to ask something of me?"

"We're here quite by accident." Jettie answered, popping to the side like an anemone. "We were just swimming along and got hungry and Flottie started looking for food."

Jettie glanced at Flottie as if the other eel-maid might pick up the story. When she didn't, Jettie flicked her tail and popped to the other side. "Then she smelled food—crabs to be exact—and her nose led us to this den."

She flicked her tail again and twirled, her arms stretched out to indicate my home. As if I didn't know whose den her story referenced. With another flick, she was back within arms-reach, her smile wide, showcasing her small but sharp teeth. If it had been anyone else, I might have assumed that was a threat. But her demeanor exuded only joy and a stimulating innocence as she continued. "The den was so messy, with so many crabs wandering around, we assumed it was abandoned and decided to enjoy some lunch."

Her expression fell, and her shoulders hunched as she drifted even closer. Her voice was small with regret and she hugged herself. "We had no idea this was your den. Please forgive us, Mr. Sea Witch. It was an accident. Honest. We didn't mean to intrude or anger you or make you think we wanted anything from you."

Jettie drifted back. No, wait. She didn't drift; Flottie wound an arm around Jettie's waist and pulled until she melted against Flottie's front, their tails entangling again. The move was decidedly comforting. Protective, even, except that Jettie was still very much within my tentacle's reach. And my tentacles yearned to reach for her. To wrap around her like she was a sack of scallops to covet. Would she yield to my embrace as easily as she had Flottie's? If I was quick enough, I could very likely snatch Jettie away from Flottie.

But I wasn't a monster, and Jettie wasn't a thoughtless thingamabob to fight over.

"Forgive us if we're a little awe-struck." Flottie's voice soothed me more effectively than any potion I could mix. "We've both admired you for many years."

That declaration shocked me back to reality. No one *admired* me. Tolerated me, likely. Feared me, probably. Wanted me for what I could do for them, definitely. But admired me?

Absolutely not. "I've never seen either of you before. How can you possibly claim to admire me?"

"How can we admire you?" Jettie perked up, her mouth open in an adorable *O*. She flailed her hands around as if that was explanation enough, though she remained in Flottie's embrace. "How can we *not* admire you?"

Flottie chuckled and shot an indulgent smile to her...um, friend...before explaining further. "You're Ursule the Sea Witch. Ursule who solved the Great Urchin Crisis. Ursule who brought the coral of the dead Tirulian Reef back to its former glory. Ursule who saved the Atlantian Royal Conductor from falling into the boiling waters of a hydrothermal vent. Ursule who answered Prince Eric's wish to find a princess worthy of his love."

I swallowed my snort of laughter, which caused me to choke. Their faces were both so sincere, so earnest, I couldn't bring myself to crush their belief I had single-tentacledly solved any of those crises. That would be cruel. Like telling a mer-child Sandy Claws, the giant red crab who traveled the oceans giving gifts to good little creatures, wasn't real.

By the Tides, I wasn't that much of a monster.

Flottie and Jettie would learn soon enough that I had been only loosely connected to the so-called accomplishments they'd listed. Except for the last one; that had been all on Prince Eric, Princess Ariel, and a cosmic fate far more powerful than me.

Yet hearing my name associated with so many great happenings was a heavy stroke to my ego, even if I was the only one who knew there were reasonable explanations which made my supposedly amazing contributions much less awe-inspiring.

For example, a few seasons ago, I had mentioned in passing to a pod of spiny lobsters and a cast of nearby crabs that the urchins were plentiful; the crustaceans had gorged until the urchin population was again manageable. The formerly dead Tirulian Reef had suffered from overpopulation of sea worms and barnacles, which I'd been happy to glut myself on while hiding from a particularly fanatic admirer; without the worms and barnacles, the rest of its inhabitants had been eager to return. Saving the Royal Conductor had been more of an accident than anything. I'd been reaching for a small lobster for dinner, but had snagged the conductor instead. Miffed I'd missed my dinner, I tossed him away—from me, and apparently from the vent—but he'd decided I'd acted heroically and made sure everyone knew about it.

Curse the Tides, I couldn't diminish my reputation even when I tried.

I glanced at Flottie and Jettie, who both wore expressions of adoration so sincere, my gut hollowed with guilt. I shook my head and my tentacles curled. "That's all very flattering. But I tend to grate on everyone if given enough time."

Time we didn't have because we were still in my den, and they were passing through. If their words were to be believed, they'd happened upon me by accident, and would likely continue on their way soon.

Why did the thought of them leaving fill me with despair? I was a lone cecaelia male—had been all my life except as an eggling—and my cranky nature ensured my solitary lifestyle continued. A few potential suitors had tried to brave my temperament, and failed. If I had to put up with unwelcome company for any length of time, there was no description for how irascible I could become.

Still, the thought of these two mers leaving unsettled me for some reason I couldn't parse.

I coughed away the tightening in my throat and motioned toward the entrance. "Well. Thank you for greatly diminishing my annoying crab infestation. I don't want to keep you from continuing on your journey."

Flottie and Jettie shared a look, Jettie's face pinched with worry and Flottie's fell with regret. Their arms entwined and they held each other as if silently consoling one another over something. Mers usually appearing dejected when I denied their requests, but this was new. I hadn't denied these two eel-maids anything, because they hadn't asked anything of me.

Jettie lifted her head from Flottie's shoulder and looked at me, her expression disappointed as if I'd already told her *no*. Which, okay, I was probably going to do. But my reputation obviously preceded me, so they should know I never willingly— or at least enthusiastically—accepted requests for wish fulfillment. Jettie nibbled her bottom lip, and for a moment I wished my teeth were testing the plumpness of those lips. Fortunately, her voice pulled me from those wayward thoughts. "Mr. Sea Witch, we don't mean to intrude in your home. But we've traveled a long distance. We're tired and finding another empty cave could take a long time."

She didn't continue. There was a question—a request—in her voice, but she didn't ask it. Waiting for the ask was as annoying as actually hearing it, and I might have been a little too hungry to be nice. Either way, my emotions got the best of me. I snapped. "Well, spit it out. What does any of that have to do with me?"

Jettie cringed into Flottie's welcoming body and hid her face against her... friend's?... neck. Yes, I was a complete blobfish for being so churlish. And while it was well within my character to be thus, a ping of regret for how my tone affected this innocent mer stabbed one of my hearts. Or maybe I'd eaten a bad prawn and this was indigestion. Maybe I was dying.

No. I just felt bad for being unnecessarily mean.

Flottie looked at me, her expression forlorn, but not accusing. I'd hurt Jettie and yet Flottie didn't seem angry about it at all. In fact, she appeared... resigned. As if my boorish treatment was something they were accustomed to. But I'd never met them before this day, which meant someone else had treated them with the same level of irritation and dismissal. Perhaps more than some_one_. Maybe *someones*. And the thought that others had treated these two lovely eel-maids in the same manner I treated everyone angered me for some inexplicable reason.

Wait, was I... empathizing with them? Was I feeling... regret for my behavior?

By the Tides, I was definitely dying.

"Mr. Sea Witch, please forgive us." Flottie's silky voice soothed my impending death. "You asked what we wanted of you. Well, I guess you could say we want a place to stay. At least for this night. We promise not to bother you. We won't even talk to you if that's what you want. We'll just curl up in a corner of your den and sleep, then we'll leave tomorrow."

I stared at the two mers for several moments, not sure I'd heard them correctly. "So, you want to sleep on the hard, cold floor of my den for a night until I kick you out."

Jettie tensed at my words and I would swear I heard her whimper against Flottie's shoulder. Flottie immediately shook her head. "You won't need to kick us out. We'll leave before then. Don't worry, we don't stay where we're not wanted. I'm merely asking for this one night because we've traveled so far to find a safe place to rest. But we'll understand if you deny us."

Deny their simple request to sleep in a corner of my den? A colony of crabs had moved into my den without even so much as a *please* or a *thank you* for the food I inadvertently provided them. They didn't acknowledge me, even when I ate their brethren. Mers constantly sought me out to ask me for wish fulfillment, and paid no heed to whether or not I wanted the responsibility. These two had stumbled upon my den and knew I was well within my rights to kick them out at any moment. But for once, I hesitated to respond. Something about my typical tentacle-jerk denial of any request seemed harsh. Cruel, even.

"One night in my den." I huffed a small, disbelieving chuckle, which was an odd sensation because I so rarely laughed, and shook my head. "Ladies, of all the requests and wishes I've ever received, that one has to be the most underwhelming."

Rather than continue to hover near my own entrance, I plucked up the forgotten bag of scallops and deposited it on my bed platform. Then, I pondered the spacious den. Other than my bed, which was set along an arched wall creating a cozy little sleeping nook, there wasn't much else to the space. A pile of things I'd scavenged like small bowls and shells and pretty rocks lined the far wall. A heap of kelp tumbled off my bed platform to the floor. My bed was large enough to host the Atlantian army, but I didn't think these eel-maids would appreciate a lascivious invitation to join me there. Besides, I didn't really know these mer-eels. There was every possibility they'd try to make a snack out of my soft, clever appendages while I slept.

So, I gathered the kelp and transferred it to a corner, fluffing the long, crushed strands until they made a softish nest for two. "There." I waved at the pile and turned to the eel-maids, who had silently watched me as if I might sprout a second head. "I can't offer you accommodations to rival the Atlantian palace, but this should be comfortable enough for you to sleep on."

"You're… You mean you're actually going to let us spend the night?" Jetties soft, incredulous whisper, paired with the obvious tremble in her lower lip, nearly broke my hearts. I wasn't offering them much of anything. A little spot on my floor and some old kelp I no longer needed. I hadn't even offered them my sleeping platform because I wasn't that nice. Yet they both looked like I'd offered them a bedroom worthy of royalty.

Something clogged my throat so I had to cough to clear it. "Well, I mean… I often help unfortunate merfolk, like yourself." I ignored that obvious lie—which didn't feel like a lie at the moment—and shrugged, unsure what else to say. "You both did such a good job of reducing my crab infestation. Letting you sleep here is the least I could do."

"But, you didn't ask us to eat the crabs. You didn't even invite us in." Flottie pointed out. "So you shouldn't feel obligated to repay us."

She had a point. One I would have normally made myself to keep from having to owe anybody anything, because being in someone's debt was worse than being asked to bring someone's dead lover back to life. I threaded my fingers through my short white hair and scratched the back of my neck. Oddly enough, I didn't suffer under the weight of any obligation. I wasn't in their debt, nor were they in mine. There wasn't anything transactional about my offer to let them sleep here.

It was... the right thing to do.

Curse the Tides, was I becoming—*shudder*—considerate?

"Letting you sleep here for a night isn't a hardship or an obligation. I'm merely thankful for the service you provided me, albeit unwittingly." I waved it all away with an agitated tentacle... Their concerns... My weird, new moral compass... Even my odd invitation for them to stay. Surely I was just hungry and everything would get back to normal after a satisfying meal of scallops and a good night's sleep.

Turning my back to the eel-maids in an effort to cut off any possible objections and maybe somehow halt this bizarre twist to my surly character, I climbed atop my platform. My tentacles lifted the sack of scallops and set it next to me, working the knot around the bag while I contemplated my next decision. I should offer to share my dinner with the eel-maids. That would be the *right* thing to do, dammit, but I'd already stepped leagues out of my comfort zone by allowing them to stay. Plus, they'd already gorged themselves on crab, and a few lucky survivors still skittered across the floor if the maids wanted more. Besides, these scallops were my payment for future services promised. I was the only one who could craft the love lotion, so I should be the only one to enjoy the—

I sighed, water passing over my gills. My pathetic excuses flagged, leaving me with the uncomfortable reality of my selfishness. It wouldn't kill me to share a few scallops with these eel-maids. The words dragged out of my mouth as if pulled by some unseen force. "Would you like to join me, ladies?" Curse the Tides, that sounded like I'd invited them to share my bed. I quickly shook the bag so the scallops rattled against each other. "For dinner. There's plenty for all of us."

Not quite the truth. I could easily eat the entire bag's worth. But I certainly wouldn't die from starvation if they enjoyed a few scallops with me. However, they didn't. In fact, one of them, probably Jettie if the lilting, sunny pitch indicated anything, giggled—*giggled!*—at my offer. Had she clawed my tentacle, I wouldn't have been as shocked. I pulled the bag back and turned away. Served me right for trying to be nice. I obviously had no practice with that skill, and should stick to—

"Flottie, he called us *ladies*." Jettie's high voice, filled with wonder, whispered behind me. Flottie's sultry chuckled followed.

I frowned at them over my shoulder, confused and not liking the feeling one bit. "Why shouldn't I call you *ladies*?" Were they mocking me for being nice? "Why does that make me such a funny joke?"

"We don't think you're a joke, Mr. Sea Witch. Not at all." Flottie shook her head, her expression one of sincerity, not condemnation. "It's only that no one else has ever called us *ladies* before."

Well, wasn't I an idiot. "Of course, you're right. They would call you by your names. Not that we've made formal introductions, but I'm aware your names are Flottie and Jettie. I'll be sure to—"

"No one calls us by our names, either." Jettie interrupted, then hid her face against Flottie's shoulder.

I frowned. What else would anyone call these two lovely—

"They call us trash." Flottie answered my unspoken question. Her fists were clenched at her sides, her jaw set in a determined line, yet she held her head high and met my gaze without flinching. "They call us trash and throw us away and ignore us."

I whirled to face them fully, my independent tentacles blessedly as focused on these two mers as the rest of me. Flottie and Jettie held each other close, but their familiarity made little sense. Mer-eels were solitary creatures, like me. They didn't require a community, a school, or even a partner. The fact these two had paired up in what appeared to be a long-term sort of way... well, it defied logic. At the very least, it defied their nature.

Although working together went against mer-eel nature, it seemed to benefit these two. Rather than each having to find food and shelter and safety, they could share the responsibility and reward of hunting dinner while also protecting one another. The idea was actually very logical, and while I questioned my own recent contra-nature behavior, I respected Flottie and Jettie for trying something different than what their kind normally abided.

But that didn't explain why anyone should consider them trash.

"*They*? Meaning your fellow mer-eels? Or...?"

"Everyone." Jettie's voice was muffled against Flottie's shoulder. She twisted her head enough to look at me. "We've traveled all over to find a place we could call home, yet we can't outswim our reputation."

Flottie pulled Jettie closer. I hadn't noticed before, but the little slip of an eel-maid trembled in her friend's arms. They both looked akin to when I'd practically shoved them out my den door in my haste to be alone. In my haste to suffer their inevitable departure.

My brilliant mind connected the dots. Finally. "When I said earlier that I didn't want to keep you from continuing your journey, did you think I was throwing you out?"

Jettie turned her head from Flottie's chest, but her gaze didn't meet mine. Her shoulder lifted as if in a shrug, but even I—in my recent, rare state of obtuseness—discerned the motion was more a sign of tension than indifference. "Yes, we did. But that's okay, it happens all the time. You aren't the first to want us gone."

Scallops forgotten. My solitary nature forgotten. The ramifications of my words also forgotten. I scrabbled off the platform and over to where they huddled, stopping barely a breath away from them, my chest heaving with some sort of vehement outrage I'd never before known except when anyone asked anything of me, only this time it was directed at all the unknown creatures who had ever slighted these two eel-maids. I blurted. "I might not be the first or even the middle, but, by the Tides, I will be the last. You both are welcome in my den for as long as you wish. And if you choose to leave, you are welcome back anytime you want to return. I'm crusty and cranky and impossible to live with, but I will never throw you out. You. Are. Not. Trash."

Jettie's trembles turned to quakes and she threw her arms around my shoulders. Normally, I'd cringe and squirm to get away from the contact, but not this time. I wrapped my arms around her slender body and held her tight, as if by willpower alone I could erase all the hurt she'd suffered at the whims of others. I looked over her shoulder at Flottie, who's expression was bleak with utter gratitude. Like no one had ever done anything nice for either of them, and she wasn't sure how to react much less how to cover it up with a shred of dignity.

Or maybe that was just my own attempt to understand the emotions tumbling through me like a rock slide.

"You aren't crusty or cranky." Jettie's quiet declaration murmured against the side of my neck where she'd buried her face, and I felt her words tickle down through my suckers to the tips of my tentacles.

Flottie crowded against Jettie's backside and reached around her to rest her hands on my sides and squeeze. Her eyelids dipped and she tilted her head like she was going to kiss me even with her friend cushioned between us. Of their own volition, my tentacles slithered up her back and pulled her closer, cupping her head. And for once I wasn't opposed to the intimate proximity.

By the Tides, I wanted to kiss one of both of these eel-maids more than I wanted my scallops. And that truth shocked me back to reality. I'd just met them, yet I'd opened my den to them more readily than if they were family, held one flush against my aroused body, and was moments from pressing my attentions on the other.

The hazy moment was interrupted by my stomach rumbling its hunger loud enough for the Atlantian palace to hear. Flottie pulled away and Jettie giggled as she released her grip on me.

"We've kept you from your dinner long enough, Mr. Sea Witch." She smiled as she drifted into Flottie's embrace, and I most assuredly experienced jealousy at that sight. I was jealous they were as comfortable touching one another as I was *not* being touched by anyone. Or, at least not being touched by anyone but these two mers. The last few moments were enough to question the validity of my claim to not want any physical contact.

The possibility of more physical contact with these two *ladies* heated me like a hydrothermal vent.

With an awkward nod to them, I returned to my bed—the platform now feeling strangely empty and cold—and to my scallops. One glance to the eel-maids proved they'd bedded down in the kelp pile, their arms and tails entwined, whispering quietly to each other. Normally, whispers in dark corners were suspicious, and I would assume the participants were plotting something. I didn't have nearly enough tentacles to count the times mers have tried to sabotage me into doing their bidding, as if they could out-smart me. Fortunately, I was irascible enough to avoid being guilted or blackmailed.

But the whispers drifting my way didn't strike me as suspicious. Rather the opposite: they were soft and comforting.

Was this how the two eel-maids said good-night to each other? What would life be like if I had someone whispering comforting words to me? I thought of the mermaid from the reef, the one who'd bartered with scallops. If she'd tried whispering anything in my ear, I likely would have shoved her into the next sea. Just the thought of her being near me made me tense and my stomach churn. But the thought of Flottie and Jettie near me, whispering in my ears, maybe even touching me, tangling their tails with my tentacles, running their hands over my—

I coughed and yanked my thoughts back to my dinner. One grateful hug did not mean these two mers wanted anything physical with me... more than likely, they were in a committed relationship with each other. And hugging me had simply been because they were overjoyed by my proclamation. Or they were just touch-feely kind of mers who forgot others might not be the same.

Regardless, I was way too aroused at the mere thought of platonic physical contact with them.

My stomach rumbled again, reminding me I was supposed to be eating dinner. I grabbed a scallop out of the bag, my suckers winning the battle against its hinge muscle, and laid the shell open to reveal the succulent mollusk contents. Using my tongue and it's conveniently rasping chitinous texture, I scraped all the sweet flesh from the shell into my mouth, chewing slowly and savoring the taste and texture. I repeated this process with the next three, my tongue scouring the inner surface of the shell to dislodge every bit of delicious scallop.

As my tongue swiped at my lips to gather the last bit of juice there, a soft moan from the corner caught my attention. Flottie and Jettie were still wrapped around one another on the kelp pile. Jettie squirmed in Flottie's embrace, but not because she was uncomfortable or trying to escape. The curvier eel-maid held her in a loose hug, one hand cupping a breast, her fingers rolling the nipple, while the other hand was lower, those fingers brushing against the pink anemone that had attached the front of Jettie's tail.

Huh. I don't remember her having an anemone stuck to her—

I mentally smacked myself for being dense. That wasn't an actual anemone. The delicate petals of Jettie's sex were swelled, wafting in the water, having unfurled from the recesses of her sheath with Flottie's encouragement, a sheen of slick mucus clouding the immediate vicinity and coating Flottie's hand.

Fuck the Tides, the ladies were pursuing their pleasure in my den, where I'd invited them to stay, forgetting the fact all the creatures of Atlantia except me were open and prolific with their sexual pursuits. What else would these two mers do at night but fuck? And here I was, making love to my dinner and no one else.

Little wonder I was such a crusty curmudgeon.

Jettie moaned again, threading her fingers through Flottie's hair and gazing directly at me. I didn't breathe. Was she mad I watched? Embarrassed? Should I turn away and continue with my meal, even though the thought of my scallops didn't quite entice as they had moments before.

"Mr. Sea Witch, please don't stop eating." Jettie's voice was high and keening, her expression dazed as she arched against Flottie's palm. "Your tongue… your tongue looks amazing."

Flottie murmured her agreement, her gaze on me as she caressed her friend. "I imagine it feels amazing, too."

She rolled Jettie's sex between her fingertips and Jettie moaned and shuddered.

By the Tides, this was the most erotic thing I'd ever witnessed, and I'd seen plenty of mers fucking. Without taking my gaze from the scene on the kelp, I lifted another scallop to my mouth and flicked the tip of my tongue against my dinner's firm flesh. Jettie tugged Flottie's hand off her breast and sucked the fingers into her mouth, moaning as she watched me tongue the mollusk like it was her silky fronds. Soon, I was undulating my tongue against the helpless scallop while Flottie plunged two fingers into Jettie's hole in time to my licks, her thumb rubbing mercilessly at Jettie's swollen sex. Flottie thrust her hips against Jettie's backside, keening at the rhythmic friction on her own sex.

My cock was hard as an oyster shell, desperate for some friction. But I ignored my throbbing desire, too intent on licking the scallop and wishing it was one of the ee-maids. Too focused on watching the ladies strive toward their climaxes to care about my own. A tentacle wrapped itself around my cock, and I quickly swiped it off. This moment was about the ladies. And… well, hopefully impressing them with my tongue skills.

We eye fucked each other like this until Jettie cried out her release, arching back against Flottie, who followed, moaning into Jettie's hair. Their juices dissipated into the surrounding water and my tentacles quivered, my suckers as desperate as my mouth for a taste of their special flavors.

The ladies slowly relaxed, their sated limbs still entwined, settling further into the kelp pile as slumber claimed them. I watched until their deep breaths were the only sound in my den. My arousal still raged, unrequited. I could take myself in hand or tentacle and finish in moments, I was already so close. But it wouldn't satisfy. Even after knowing these ladies for such a short period of time, their influence on my life was potent. More powerful than my base need for release. If they chose to stay, and every night promised to be a repeat of their passion and my sexual self-restraint, that sounded oceans more meaningful than my lonely life before.

But if they chose to leave, and my normal life resumed, that sounded like the worst form of torture.

Even so, I'd prefer to not spend the rest of my life in a state of sexually frustrated celibacy. If they stayed, we would have to work out a schedule. Or I'd have to find another secret location to see to my own needs.

I quietly tucked the few remaining scallops beside my bed.

They would make a tasty morning snack, even though I longed for a snack of a different sort. Then, I settled on my side and stared at the back wall, trying to ignore both my aching cock and my curious fascination with the eel-maids. In the quiet of the night, the few remaining crabs braved the floor of my den, their legs clicking their progress. Between the familiar noise, paired with the comforting sound of two particular eel-maids sleeping behind me, I soon eased into sleep plagued with sensual dreams of mer-eel touches and the music of their cresting pleasure.

When I woke the next day, exhausted and sexually frustrated from a fitful night filled with erotic images, Flottie and Jettie still slept in each other's arm. Their peaceful faces, relaxed and youthful, melted my hearts. If they'd truly been searching for any length of time for a home, a safe place to rest, then they were likely exhausted. I didn't dare wake them up, even though my tentacles wriggled with the need to touch them and fluff the meager kelp pile.

I would go get them more kelp. Fresh kelp. That was good, they would like that. While I was out, I'd gather ingredients for the lotion and some food. Lots of food. I bet they would wake up famished even though they'd devoured so many crabs yesterday. They said they'd been traveling for a long time, so they likely hadn't had time or opportunity for more than the barest sustenance. I slid off my bed and hurried silently toward the door. Before I reached the opening, my tentacles veered closer to the ladies, to my surprise. Apparently, my tentacles had grabbed the leftover scallops and now laid the nibbles near enough to Flottie and Jettie they would hopefully see and know they were welcome to enjoy the small offering.

My independent tentacles were often at odds with my own wishes. I had always assumed that, while my intellect solved the problems for what seemed all of Atlantia, my tentacles acted on my more instinctive needs such as gathering food, avoidance of touch, and escaping unwanted attention. But at this moment, in our mutual need to care for the two eel-maids, we acted as a singular entity.

The bit of breakfast laid out for the ladies, my tentacles hurried me from the den and toward our first destination: the kelp forest. While the closest one was all the way on the other side of the low plains, once I arrived, I quickly gathered a large, fresh batch of the long strands. In truth, I was tactless with my selection, more concerned with quantity and speed than in ensuring my harvest didn't adversely impact the vast field of the plant.

"I'll return soon and spend time reseeding to replace what I took." I promised to the swaying plants, even though they couldn't hear me or respond. It was more a promise to myself. Even the brainless jellyfish with its simple cluster of nerve cells knew not to be greedy with the bounty of our waters.

Hastening back to my den, I arrived just as the ladies dined on the last of the scallops. I paused at the sight, unsure how they might react to my presence after last night. After the sex that hadn't been sex but had been absolutely sexual and yet so much more—

"Mr. Sea Witch! You didn't leave us!" Jettie's joyous welcome washed away my hesitation. I had no more than a few tentacles inside the den when she threw herself at me, wrapping her arms around my neck like she had yesterday. Her trajectory and happy squeal nearly knocked me off-balance and my tentacles clung to her to keep her safe. And to keep her flush against my body.

I laughed—*laughed!*—at her enthusiasm. "Of course, I didn't leave you. This *is* my den, remember?"

Flottie approached, much like she had last night, but her somber, hesitant expression tempered my own good humor. Before I could question her reservation, she offered me a tentative smile. "We worried you'd changed your mind. You didn't say anything last night about staying here with us in your den. And when we woke up to find you gone…"

She didn't finish her thought. She didn't have to. I knew exactly what she meant. Rather than offer her bland words or empty promises, my tentacles merely held up the bundle of kelp I'd hauled here. "You both were sleeping so soundly, I didn't want to wake you. So, I slipped out this morning to get you fresher bedding. It will be so much more comfortable than the crumpled leaves I offered you last night."

They both gasped as I pulled the enormous strands of kelp fully into the den. The leafy plant was so fresh and full, it took up half the den and looked nothing like any sort of bedding, but it would compress nicely. Jettie grabbed a strand, her eyes wide sand dollars of awe. Flottie fingered the soft leaves with a reverence usually saved for royalty.

Had no one ever done anything nice for either of them? My frustration with the entirety of the ocean burst forth and I shook a kelp end with more force than required, but with the intended result. A wide selection of creatures that often lived among kelp and had stuck to the leaves even as I hurried back to my den tumbled to the floor. Scud, bristle worms, prawns, snails, and a few unlucky stunned rockfish. I smiled and waved at the offering. "Breakfast is served."

In case either of the eel-maids were too stricken by my supposed generosity, I popped a bristle worm into my mouth and crunched away. They weren't as tasty as my scallops, but much easier to eat.

Thankfully neither Flottie nor Jettie balked at making a meal of the kelp hold-ons. Between the three of us, the strands were soon clear of critter life, and we lounged together on the soft bedding of fresh leaves, our bellies painfully full and a comfortable stream of conversation drifting between us.

Jettie rolled to face me, her expression contented. She reached out and lightly traced her fingertips down my shoulder, her voice soft and dreamy. "Mr. Sea Witch, can it always be like this?"

"What do you mean?" Her question was vague enough I didn't know how to answer.

Flottie raised up from her prone position and also faced me, the tip of her tail resting against my hip. "She means this calm. This easy. Can we always be this comfortable with one another?"

"You're asking me to predict the future." I rolled a kelp tendril around my finger, wishing it was a lock of hair from either of them. "I'm smart, but I'm not all-knowing. For what it's worth, I can't imagine a scenario where we wouldn't be this way. Does that help?"

I ignored the discomfort I would inevitably experience every time they sexually satisfied one another while I tried not to be an overly lecherous and obvious onlooker.

"Our reputation follows us everywhere." Flottie spoke softly, her smooth voice like a caress even though I bristled at her words. "Being around us will defile your reputation and scare other mers away. You will come to resent us for that."

I chuckled at the absurdity of that statement. "Resent you for ensuring Atlantians stay away from me? That sounds like a dream—" my humor evaporated when Flottie's words finally registered. "Wait, you mean your reputation as trash? I don't understand why would anyone think that of you, much less why it would be so pervasive as to follow you here."

This logic was a dense jungle of spiny urchins in my brain.

Jettie sunk further into the kelp, paling so her dark spots were nearly as light as the rest of her. Flottie met my gaze, her expression pinched and desolate. "You truly haven't heard about us? The heartless eel princess who stabbed her intended husband and the ungrateful servant who ran away with her?"

I was an intelligent problem-solver, but I wasn't social enough to keep on top of the latest gossip. Guess I'd missed some juicy stuff.

In answer to her question, I could only gape, and shake my head. "I don't recall ever having heard that story."

Jettie crossed her arms over her chest, her expression dour. Almost sullen. She muttered just loudly enough for me to hear. "Others will have heard. And if they see you with us, they will question your judgement, Mr. Sea Witch. Which means they'll stop honoring you like you deserve. You should send us on our way before anyone learns you were nice to us."

My tentacles wrapped around her waist and pulled her up to face me. My tentacles similarly wrapped around Flottie so she understood I spoke to both of them. "The mers of Atlantia don't honor me. They might fear me. They certainly think I can solve all of their problems. But that is not the same as honoring me. And if a mer decides to question my judgement because I am seen with you, then that's one less mer I'll be bothered to help. So, you two will in no way impact my life except to make me happier than I've ever been."

A body slammed into me and warm arms squeezed my shoulders. Flottie tipped her face against the side of mine. Jettie squirmed out of my grip and did the same, her body pressed against my front and her arms around my torso. They held me tightly and my own tentacles reciprocated the desperate gesture. Both mers whispered thank-yous in such an earnest tone, my hearts melted. My meager offer to let them stay and my cheeky refusal to let the possible disdain of others I cared so little about change my mind… well, it shouldn't mean so much. Certainly not this much. These two eel-maids reacted like I'd crowned them queens of the ocean and offered them unlimited power, when all I'd done was be nice to them.

And they didn't even know just how much I detested being nice.

"Mr. Sea Witch." Flottie's sultry voice was in my ear as her hands slid down my torso. "May I kiss you?"

My hearts jumped to my throat and I turned to look at her.

Her deep color had darkened further with desire and she stared at my lips. Was she truly aroused? Or was this another way to thank me for the meager kindness I'd offered them?

And why was my throat suddenly dry?

"Flottie, you are under no obligation to offer my anything." The words poured from my mouth even as my body scream *Yes! Kiss me!* "I did not invite you to stay with any expectation of repayment. Neither did I bring the kelp or feed you with the intention of making you beholden to me in any way. The three of us are here by our own choice and free will. No payment. No expectation. No contract."

She blinked at me, her eyes wide and her lush lips parted in shock. Or, dare I hope, desire?

Rational thought gave way to the delicious sensations these two maids elicited. Their bodies flush against mine. Their hands explored my torso and tentacles, leaving trails of pebbled flesh and blazing a path of need straight to my cock. My tentacles had already coiled around the two maids, pulling them tight against me, my suckers tasting them, exploring them. They were more delicious than an endless supply of scallops, and euphoria spread through me. Euphoria, and a desperation to kiss one or both of these maids.

My big brain clouded and my voice quavered as I struggled against my own desire to ensure they understood. "I demand nothing from either of you. And I expect even less. But…" I swallowed to hold back my swelling desire just enough to refrain from forcing my attention on them. "But if you ladies are amenable to allowing a third mer to interject himself into your relationship, I would very much like for you to kiss me."

Jettie giggled against my neck, her fingertips walking up and down my spine. "Mr. Sea Witch, that sure is a fancy way to say *yes.*"

I huffed a soft laugh at Jettie's observation and tried to shrug. "It's a talent that I always have possessed."

Flottie merely stared at my lips, and the sight nearly sent me over the edge. "What other talents do you have?" Her tongue swiped across her mouth.

"Let me show you." I managed before my lips covered hers. She kissed me back with a fervor I'd never known from another lover. As if she truly desired me. Me, the crustiest, crabbiest, most unlovable mer in all Atlantia. My tongue slipped into her mouth, dancing with hers as my tentacles twined around her limbs and tail, sucking and tasting and plumping.

Jettie's mouth covered my chest and stomach with hungry kisses, her tongue and sharp teeth nibbling their way down to where my cock emerged from my slit, throbbing and insistent in the warm water surrounding us. Her dainty hands cupped me and shuttled along my length. Her tongue flicked the flared tip and flattened along the angled ridges leading down to the rows of tiny suckers. We both moaned.

I tore my mouth from Flottie's and pulled Jettie up to my lips, equally as desperate to kiss her. She wrapped her tail around the tentacles that held her against me, moaning against my tongue, her hands seeking my cock again. I pinned Flottie to my side, my tentacles sneaking around to her front where her band of kelp had fallen from her chest. While my hands were busy exploring Jettie, my tentacles covered Flottie, squeezing her heavy breasts and plucking at her delicious nipples until she arched and moaned. The little suckers at the tips of my tentacles found where her silky sex folds had unfurled and played with her delicate fronds. She arched against me, her throaty moans an erotic song to my ears.

Both of these ladies deserved languid kisses, meaningful caresses, day-long lovemaking. They deserved a lover who would step aside and be content to watch them enjoy one another. But that wasn't me. I was greedy with need. I couldn't get enough of their sounds and their flavors and the way they squirmed against my tentacles. I wanted to devour them until we all screamed our climaxes to the great blue.

Easing my mouth from Jettie's, I kissed a frantic path along her jawline and neck, working my way down her body much like she had mine earlier, until her sweet pink anemone was eye-level. I latched on, licking and flicking it with my tongue, sucking it further into my mouth, my tongue's rasping texture merciless against her engorged petals. She cried out, fisting my hair and wrapping her tail around my head as if to keep it there.

As if I would stop.

Well, I would stop. But only at their command.

While I gorged on Jettie's delicious sex, my tentacle tips wriggled their way through Flottie's silky fronds and teased at her entrance. Her guttural groans—low vibrations that merged like a symphony with Jettie's high mewls—grew and she licked and kissed wherever her mouth could reach. My body. Jettie's body. My cock. She swallowed my length deep into her hot mouth and I moaned at the spike of pleasure that shot to my suckers.

My tentacles took over where my mouth had been, tickling and wriggling against Jettie's engorged sex, dipping in and out of her channel in time with Flottie's bobbing head. I drifted up so I could suck on Jettie's sweet little pearled nipples. Any tentacles not otherwise engaged slithered around the two maids and tickled their tiny back entrance. Mers weren't as supple in this hole as other orifices, but it was still a erogenous playground, and both maids cried out in pleasure as my tentacles stretched thin and wiggled inside.

Mouths and hands and bodies and tentacles rubbed and caressed in a desperate rhythm. Moans and mewls echoed off the den walls. My release was moments away, so I tugged Flottie off of my cock. By the Tides I wanted to come, but not before these two beauties found their pleasure. I replaced my cock in her mouth with my tongue. Jettie pushed in and took over the kiss.

"Taste how delicious he is." Flottie demanded of her friend before shoving her tongue down Jettie's welcoming throat. I watched their feverish kiss from the corner of my eyes as I kissed and nibble on someone's throat. Then someone else's breast. And back to someone's earlobe. I had no idea which one of them I kissed and caressed and ground my cock against. My tentacles were equally indiscriminate, curling and writhing in whatever orifice they could find, suctions tasting sleek flesh and soft skin and savory channels. The water around us clouded with our various secretions, heavy with the scent of our mutual arousal and tastier than any banquet. We were a mindless mass of bodies straining toward our climax.

"Fuck her." Jettie demanded in my ear. "Fuck her so good she screams, Mr. Sea Witch."

For such a slight, slender eel-maid, she sure was bossy. Who was I to tell either of these maids *no*? The only need throbbing in every cell of my body was the need to indulge them. Satisfy them. Bring them as much pleasure as I was physically capable of.

I didn't mind Jettie's bossiness in the least. Not even when she gripped my writhing cock and unnecessarily helped it to the entrance of Flottie's slick channel. Like any of my tentacles, my cock was adept at finding it's intended destination, and once there, it wormed its undulating way inside.

Flottie arched into me when I was fully seated, her sheath clenching my undulating cock and her eyes rolling back. Jettie drifted behind her, an echo of their position from the night before, and plumped Flottie's breasts, offering them up for me. I was too intent on watching the bliss on their faces, so my tentacles accepted the gift instead, suckers clamping on and writhing against Flottie's puckered nipples. She shivered as I began a languid rhythm, thrusting deep and strong. My cock's flared tip with its ridges whorled against her sensitive walls and the suckers kissed everywhere else.

Flottie's expression grew slack, her mouth open as a constant chorus of moans flowed from her. She was at my mercy as I picked up the pace, the skin around my cockslit pebbling for added stimulation to her silky petals which each thrust. My tentacles continued their devotion to her breasts and rear vent. The other tentacles attended to Jettie in much the same way as she rubbed against Flottie's backside, her expression equally as elated with her rising pleasure.

A tentacle cupped the back of her head and brought her lips to mine so I could kiss her with all the passion electrifying my body everywhere the two maids touched me. I fucked Flottie and kissed Jettie and my tentacles caressed and sucked with focused attention until we were a mass of mers straining for release, crying out our desires. Flottie flung her arms around Jettie and me, screaming her climax just as Jettie cried against my mouth. I clutched them tight against me, my own release hurtling up my spine and out through all my extremities in a burst of ecstasy.

We drifted on a plume of rapture, our bodies still entwined and my tentacles still twitching, onto the soft kelp bedding. Our breaths mingled, our lips casually seeking one another for unhurried kisses. A completeness I'd never known washed over me. More than the sex, more than the orgasm. The emptiness of my life before these two eel-maids had stumbled into my den spread out behind me. Lonely. Unfulfilled. A void of meager sustenance and survival.

But the past day since I'd returned to my den with a bag of scallops proved there was more to living. More potential to my life than I'd ever known.

"Mr. Sea Witch, can we always be like this?" This time, Flottie's soft voice, her head resting on my chest and her body blanketed in my tentacles, asked the question.

By the Tides, I wanted nothing more than to answer in the affirmative. But I couldn't. Not yet.

Still, I smiled at her. "You didn't scream. Did I not fuck you as good as Jettie demanded?"

Flottie blushed, her fingers toying with my chest. She worried her bottom lip with her teeth, as if I might not like her answer. Jettied pulled her in for a quick, loud kiss, then turned her smiling face to mine. "You did. Trust me, she screamed. We were just both too busy to hear it properly, Mr. Sea Witch."

I cupped Jettie's cheek and ran my thumb along her temple. My other arm snaked around Flottie's shoulder and tenderly squeezed. "After everything we just did, I think we should be on a first name basis. I'm Ursule, not Mr. Sea Witch."

Jettie gasped in delight and Flottie sank further against me, ducking her face into my neck as if shy. I hadn't actually expected that invitation to pour from my mouth—I'd *never* invited anyone to call me by my name—but the Sharkanian army couldn't make me take back those words. I wanted these two maids in my life. I wanted the familiarity first names allowed. I wanted to feed them, love them, fuck them. I just wanted to spend my time with them, regardless of what we did.

I had an abundance of brain power and tentacles, but my life had been missing something. It had been missing two eel-maids in search of unconditional acceptance.

Without realizing it, I'd always wanted the same.

I looked down at the hopeful expression on Flottie's face. "In answer to your question, yes. Yes, we can always be like this."

They both hugged me like I'd answered their wildest dreams. Maybe I had. They'd certainly answered mine.

"If that's true, Ursule." Flottie licked her lips, her eyes glittering with mischief. "Then, it's Jettie's turn. You need to fuck her until she screams."

Words to beg for a little more recovery time were on my lips, but my tentacles had already jumped at the invitation, wrapping around the maids and delving into various holes and causing both to gasp and moan. Much to my shock, my cock had already emerged from its slit, hard and eagerly searching for Jettie's exposed fronds and the slit they hid.

For all our impatience to fuck again, this time was different. Equally as impassioned yet somehow calmer. Confident that we desired one another and a mind-blowing release awaited us all. A more leisurely exploration of one another's bodies and pleasure zones. More conversation as we made love, an exchange of compliments and breathy commands, our voices rising in volume and intensity as we surged toward our mutual climax.

Again, again, we fucked like it was our first time and our last time, then drifted in one another's arm as our bodies rested, sated from the intensity of our release, content in a way none of us had ever experienced before.

This continued over the next several days. Foraging for food, sleeping, and even my attempt to craft the love lotion I'd promised, were continually interrupted by tidal waves of passion as the ever-present need for each other would overwhelm all else. Basically, we managed to stay alive and energized just enough to make it to our next impassioned bout of lovemaking. Sometimes, I merely watched Flottie and Jettie play with each other. Sometimes, one of them would watch as I fucked the other. Most times, all three of us participated. After all, there were enough orifices and wriggling pleasure-seekers to keep us all thoroughly entertained and satisfied.

And through it all, my tentacles sought out my ladies. Touching, resting against, wriggling along, wrapping around, suckers always exploring and tasting. Often not even in a sexual, aroused manner... As if my tentacles couldn't stand to be apart from my maids for even a moment. Wanted the comfort of that smallest connection. I understood that need on a soul-deep level.

Much to my own vexation, I eventually finished the lotion and had to deliver it to the mermaid.

Jettie insisted on escorting me, convinced the mer might try her new lotion out on me, and no amount of assurances on my part swayed her. Flottie argued they should remain in the den so no one would know I'd willingly befriended them. Much less that we were lovers.

I chuckled at Jettie's jealousy, but Flottie's worry broke my hearts. I pulled both maids into my arms and nuzzled their hair. "Come with me. Both of you. I'll show you around Atlantia. You'll see that no one really wants me in the way you think. And no one cares that I've chosen to be with the two of you."

Jettie eagerly nodded. Flottie didn't look convinced, but hesitantly agreed. Funny how she'd been the confident one when I'd first found them in my den. I had no idea which of them was the heartless princess and which was the ungrateful servant, and I didn't care. They were both beautiful and amazing in my eyes, and I wanted all of Atlantia to see that.

So we set off together to find the mermaid. It didn't take long, because I knew she'd be at one of a few places—the upside of being on the alert for approaching mers was the fact I kept tabs on the habits of most Atlantians. We approached the mermaid near the community garden at the bottom of the giant silt flow, and she eyed Flottie and Jettie suspiciously as they flanked me like Prince Eric's security team often did with him.

I held out a deep shell with a large dollop of cream in its middle. "Here is the lotion I promised you." Oddly enough, my voice lacked the edge of irritation it typically held when I spoke with mers.

The mermaid stared at it for a long moment, her gaze flicking to the two eel-maids. "Took you long enough to make it."

I ground my teeth together. While I hadn't expected her to throw herself at my feet in gratitude, I also hadn't anticipated her to complain. I shrugged as if I didn't care. "Perfection takes time."

"You didn't say it would take time."

"You didn't ask. Can I assume your love interest has found

someone else? Is that why you're throwing me attitude? Is that why you haven't taken the lotion I made specifically for you?"

She flinched and hesitantly took the shell from my hand, her gaze again flicking to Jettie and Flottie. "Did they help you make this?"

I frowned. Why would that matter? My back tentacles reached out and touched each eel-maid. They both trembled, so I looked back at them. Flottie stared at the ground, hugging herself as if that would make her less noticeable. Jettie's expression was filled with rage and she glared at the mermaid in front of me. I shrugged again, as if I still didn't care, when the truth was I cared even less than before about this mermaid. If I still held the shell, I'd drop it without a single apology. Maybe I should snatch the shell back and demand she pay more for the sheer inconvenience of it all and her own rudeness.

Instead, I answered calmly. "You didn't seem to care about the lotion-making process before. Why are you questioning it now? How long it takes, who is involved. Do you doubt the lotion will do what I claimed?"

I'd said the lotion would smell so good, her love interest would notice her no matter what. In truth, I'd used crushed oyster shells to scent the lotion rich with the aroma of food. What man wouldn't find a woman smelling like a meal intriguing enough to approach? Or at least notice?

If I truly wanted the lotion to smell unforgettable, I would have used the love juices of my eel-maids. That was the most alluring aroma I'd ever known, and my mouth watered at the mere thought of having that banquet on my tongue again.

Hopefully, my cock did not rouse at the thought. Sporting an erection in public was not high on my list of things to do.

The mermaid shook her head and held the shell gingerly with two fingers as if it might bite her. "I don't mean to offend, Mr. Sea Witch. It's only that everyone knows you like to be alone.

Yet here you are with these two… unsavory creatures. It makes me wonder—"

"What did you call them?" I growled. My tentacles corkscrewed in anger, my skin blazing a warning red and tensing into spikes.

The mermaid blinked like she couldn't understand my anger. "These unsavory creatures hanging on you." She pointed— *pointed!*—at Flottie and Jettie as if I didn't know they were there.

I seriously reconsidered my stance against violence. Maybe this mer was baiting me to attract her love interest, like the plan she'd originally proposed. I leaned in closer and glared at her. "Are you trying to get me to attack you so Mr. Hero will come save you? Is that why you're being so rude?"

"No, not at all." She shook her head fervently. "I don't mean to be rude. I just didn't think you knew—"

"So you think I'm stupid?"

"—that you were in the company of trash."

A tentacle shot out and squeezed her throat. She screamed as best as she could, but it came out a helpless gurgle, her fingers digging into my skin attempting to pull me off.

I squeezed harder.

Gentle hands grasped my shoulders and the tentacle choking the mermaid. Jettie's anxious voice was in my ear, and I barely heard her words over the wild thrum of my blood rushing in my veins. "Ursule, please don't. She doesn't know us except by our reputation. She only wanted to keep you safe."

My head whipped to the side, letting Jettie see my rage on her behalf. "She called you trash."

"I know. We told you that would happen." Jettie giggled, a soft, tinkling sound that lacked any offense or upset. Perhaps she and Flottie were so accustomed to being called trash, it didn't affect them. Their calm was admirable. I'd spent my life not caring about anything enough to be troubled by what others thought, but now that I finally cared about someone else, I wasn't content to hear them slandered. Jettie palmed my cheek and tugged once more on my tentacle. "She's not worth killing over it."

Her logic eased my rage and my tentacle dropped away. Just as I leaned in to kiss Jettie for being the voice of reason, another voice interrupted. A grating, pompous male voice.

"Are you in need of saving?"

A mer approached, draped in flowing robes of woven sea grass decorated with shells and coral in brilliant hues. He was flanked by several others looking equally dour.

Nodding toward the group, I addressed the mermaid, who looked shocked by the new arrivals. "Is this your love interest? It seems my time and effort with the lotion might go to waste."

He was much older than what I would have assumed a young mermaid would desire. But what did I know? I would never have thought to pair myself with anyone, much less *two* eel-maids. Yet here I was. And apparently, I would gladly wade into battle for them.

"No, Mr. Sea Witch." The mermaid shook her head so slightly, I nearly missed it. "That isn't my merman."

The mer who wasn't *the* merman huffed, and that slight sound carried a world of disdain and entitlement. "The question was aimed at my daughter."

The Mer-eel King had found my eel-maids.

Two warm, familiar bodies huddled against my back, and my tentacles instinctively coiled around them in comfort and protection. I'd just strangled a mermaid on their behalf. No telling what I'd do to protect them from whatever fate promised at the hands of this mer. My voice was ice as I addressed him. "No one needs saved. You may carry on your way."

"You will refer to His Majesty as Your Royal Highness." One of the pompous minions barked at me.

I snorted at the absurdity of it. "I don't even refer to Prince Eric as such, and he rules of all Atlantia."

"Are you always this insolent?"

"Well, I've had the odd complaint." And I couldn't care less about them, so this eel king with his sea-sized ego would just have to deal.

"Return my daughter, and I will forgive the breach of etiquette." The mer-eel king crossed his arms over his chest.

Well, wasn't he the chattiest? I couldn't win against them in a physical tousle. But I could distract and irritate enough to give my ladies a chance to escape. My tentacles gently pushed them away from me, urging them to flee while I created a diversion.

"Unfortunately, I have no idea who your daughter is." That was true; I hadn't asked and neither Flottie nor Jettie had volunteered the details, not that it mattered to me. I loved them equally.

Loved.

My three hearts hammered in my chest. I loved my eel-maids, both of them. Equally and without reservation.

And I was probably going to lose a few tentacles—or my life —to keep them safe. The tentacles would grow back. My life would not. But the two shuddering forms at my back were worth it.

So, I continued my bravado. "Perhaps I've seen your daughter, though. Does she resemble you in any way? Does she exude the same amount of arrogance? Honestly, the daughter of a *king* would likely hang out at the Atlantian palace. Have you inquired there yet?"

He wouldn't meet my gaze. "They escaped. Fled from their duties."

"They? I thought you were talking about just one daughter."

"Yes, my daughter. And some low-level servant she'd befriended. I'd intended for my daughter to marry my esteemed General." Eel-king-guy nodded to indicate a mer even older and haughtier than him. "But instead of abiding my wishes, she attacked her intended and swam off with the scullery maid."

I laughed, loud and hard. "Ouch, that has to be a hook to the lateral line, your betrothed taking such extreme measures to avoid marrying you." I sobered instantly and looked directly at both the king and the general. "How many years have you ignored your daughter's wishes, discounting her desires and preferences like she's nothing more than simple seaweed?"

The king puffed out his chest. "Marrying my general is an honor and will strengthen my legacy—"

"If he's such a great catch, then you marry him!" Flottie's furious command made us all recoil. I'd hoped she and Jettie would take advantage of my distraction and escape again. Apparently, they had not. Flottie had surged forward and now floated by my side, her hands fisted and her body shaking with emotion.

Rather than address Flottie, the king glared at me. "You will return my daughter and servant this instant!"

Somehow, spittle managed to spew from his mouth.

"Not a chance." I did not match his volume or provocation. Instead, I stated my truth with firm composure. The truth did not need to be shouted.

Plus, my calm denial really pissed him off, and the deep crimson color of his face was rather humorous.

"You don't own either of us." Jettie declared from my other side. My ladies no longer cowered behind me, and that was equal parts worrisome and admirable. I didn't want to put them in further danger, but I was also proud of them for standing up to the mer they'd been evading. "And if you ever listened to anyone else besides your little swarm of lampreys, you'd know this. You'd stop losing citizens who are tired of your selfish rules."

The king narrowed his eyes at Jettie and Flottie, his lips turning down in a sneer of disdain. "If I hadn't lost you, I would have thrown you away, anyway. You're both no better than tra-ERK!—"

My tentacle cut off whatever he was about to say, squeezing

his throat until his eyes bulged out like a Telescope Goldfish. His guards tensed, reacting too late to do anything but look mean as I leaned closer to the king, my voice quiet but hard as a horseshoe crab. "I certainly hope you weren't about to call these two ladies *trash*. Otherwise, I might have to squeeze your head right off your body."

"Left Alone! I'm so happy to see you again!"

The woman's familiar voice cut through my rage. My tentacle loosened around the king's neck as I looked around to see Princess Ariel and Prince Eric approaching with a few palace ambassadors in tow. Princess Ariel appeared ecstatic to see me, but Prince Eric eyed the mer-eels warily.

I pulled my tentacle from around the king's neck. No need to be seen trying to choke royalty to death, even though he deserved it.

As soon as the group was close enough, Princess Ariel grabbed my hand with both of hers. "It's so good to see you again, Left Alone. And in the company of these two beautiful eel-maids, you lucky dawg." She elbowed me and dropped one eyelid in a meaningful manner. I had no response; too busy wondering what a *dawg* was and why it was lucky.

The eel king whirled on the newly-arrived group and pointed at my ladies. "These two eel-maids are under my dominion and I demand they be returned."

The ambassadors appeared confused, but Prince Eric merely blinked at the eel king. "And who are you to make such a demand?"

The eel king harumphed, no doubt at the fact he wasn't afforded the honor he assumed was his due. One of his minions spoke up, voice filled with ceremonial reverence. "This is His Majesty, King Detritus the Fourth, Ruler of the Mer-Eel Kingdom."

"I know who you are, King Detritus." Eric's unruffled demeanor continued, with perhaps a smidge of annoyance like one would have with an errant child. Or I would have with most Atlantians. "My question was why you think you have the right to demand anything of me." Eric tapped the middle of his chest and his voice lowered to a loud whisper. "King of Atlantia. I kinda outrank you."

Detritus blanched. "Forgive me, Your Highness. I am merely desperate to have my daughter returned to me. She has been gone these past few years and I wish only to bring her home at long last."

I opened my mouth to call him out on his obvious lie. A mer who had been moments from calling his daughter *trash* was not the dutiful, concerned father he claimed. But Eric beat me to it, shrugging and glancing at where the ladies rested in a tangle of my tentacles, trembling in fear yet ready to finally stand up for themselves. "Ladies, are either of you being held against your will? Coerced into staying away from the mer-eel kingdom? Being forced to do or be anything you do not want? Shall I intervene on your behalf and ensure you return with King Detritus?"

Flottie and Jettie both shook their heads vehemently. Eric looked back at Detritus and merely raised an eyebrow.

Detritus's mouth gaped like a carp before he pulled himself together again. "They're just afraid their caecilian captor will punish them if they say *yes.* Which is why you must order their return to the safety of their home."

"There isn't anything that I *must do,* Detritus. Especially when the Atlantians involved have not broken any of our laws." Detritus opened his mouth, but Eric continued. "And Atlantian law usurps the laws of your kingdom."

"B-but she stabbed her husband." Detritus answered simply. As if that explained everything.

"Intended husband." Flottie, Jettie, and I all muttered the correction.

"Acts of self-defense are upheld by our laws." Princess Ariel interjected as she drifted to Eric's side. He draped an arm around her waist. "It's my understanding he was trying to force himself on her, which would be the actual crime in this case. Maybe we should put *him* on trial for assault?"

Detritus waved away Princess Ariel's interpretation of what had happened. "I'm sure it was a misunderstanding."

Her voice became an iceberg. "A misunderstanding that resulted in a woman having to stab her way to safety, then escape from the only home she's ever known and live as a fugitive for years?"

Silence reigned for several uncomfortable heartbeats before Prince Eric spoke, his demeanor seemingly oblivious to the war of words that had just been waged. "King Detritus, if ever these two eel-maids wish to return to their home for whatever reason, even if just to visit, I will assign them a security detail of royal guards to keep them safe from harm as they travel."

Then he nodded toward me and caught my gaze with a meaningful glance. "It's the least I could do, since they are married to my esteemed Royal Advisor."

"Married?!"

The shock in Detritus's voice mirrored the jolt that shot through me. Married? Why would Eric make that claim? And why did it sound like the most wonderful thing ever?

Flottie and Jettie curled into my sides, their hands clutching me, and my tentacles hugged them close. Detritus, his general, and the other sycophants were in an uproar at Eric's announcement. Enough that only I heard Jettie whisper, "Is it true, Ursule? Are we married?"

"How could we be married, and why would Prince Eric say that?" Confusion and hope battled in Flottie's quiet voice.

I wrapped them in my arms so I could look at both when I answered. "I think he's trying to help us. To help you." My own joy clashed with apprehension. What if my ladies didn't share my feelings? What if being with me was merely a pleasant respite from being fugitives? What if they didn't return my love? I swallowed hard, unsure which answer would crush me the most. "Is the thought of being married to me a good thing or a bad thing?"

Hands pulled my head down until our three foreheads touched, our noses rubbing and our lips a breath away. Jettie's hesitant smile quivered; Flottie's lips touched mine then turned upward in a joyous grin. "Being married to you would be a wish come true," she whispered.

Jettie's kiss followed and she giggled against my lips. "Best. Day. Ever."

A cough pulled my attention away from my two eel-maids, although I only lifted my gaze enough to see who had the nerve to interrupt my private conversation. Everyone looked at the three of us expectantly. Princess Ariel finally broke the silence with a knowing chuckle. "Four days holed up in your den obviously wasn't long enough to celebrate your wedding, Left Alone."

Detritus no longer looked enraged. He even managed to look a tad humble. Nervous, even. Eric swept his hand in our direction again. "Well, your highness. You are welcome to say your good-byes to your daughter before you leave to return to your home."

What? What had I missed while distracted by Flottie and Jettie's kisses?

"I… I, um, don't know which one is my daughter." Detritus admitted after a tense moment.

WHAT?!?

He shrugged, seeming only mildly embarrassed to have admitted that. "I have a dozen wives and even more mistresses. I can't keep track of all my children."

"More like can't be bothered to keep track of them." Jettie grumbled under her breath. Flottie snickered.

"Wow, you're an even worse parent than we Sharkanians." A

new voice caught everyone's attention. Mako, the Sharkanian General who had been recently appointed Chief Atlantian Officer of the Law, swam into the midst of the group and bowed to Prince Eric. "I apologize for my delay, Your Highness. Mr. Johanssen was complaining about the guppies on his lawn again."

"Thank you for coming, Mako." Eric indicated the mer-eel group. "I promised our visiting dignitaries an escort home, if you would be so kind."

Mako smiled at Detritus and entourage, flashing his three rows of serrated teeth. "General Glut and I will ensure they arrive safely." He jerked his head, and the other large Sharkanian officer floated to the other side of the group, flashing a smile so broad and so filled with teeth the mer-eels cringed and clustered together for safety.

As the Sharkanians discussed travel arrangements with Detritus, Eric and Princess Ariel drifted closer to me as if they wanted to chat. Good, because I had a crucial question for both of them. "Why would you lie about marrying us?"

Princess Ariel just smiled brighter. Eric had the grace to look guilty. "Trying to help you out, my friend."

His friend? I didn't have friends. I had mers who annoyed me. But, since he'd mentioned it, considering Eric a friend wasn't distasteful as I might have once thought. But it did lead to another crucial question. "Did you also lie about me being your esteemed royal advisor?"

He faced me, his expression solemn as a vow. "I've wanted you on my team for a long time, but never knew how to approach you about it. You're welcome to say *no*. But Atlantia would benefit from your big brain, and I could help screen the requests for your time. Especially now that you're married and will understandably be distracted by your lovely wives."

Confusion bubbled through me. "You've been king for years. Why did you wait so long to ask?"

"You're not an easy mer to approach." Eric chuckled. I nodded at the truth of his words. Had he asked me before today, I would have scoffed at the offer. "And I spent a lot of those early years trying to find my way back to my own world. It wasn't until Ariel showed up that I truly embraced what it meant to be an Atlantian. I'm making up for lost time."

My tentacles rubbed against Flottie and Jettie, understanding that particular sentiment to my core.

"And if you want an official wedding ceremony, you only need to ask." Princess Ariel added on a conspiratorial whisper.

Then she and Eric both dropped one eyelid and smiled at me.

A strange sensation that I worried might be gratitude welled up inside me. My supposed big brain could barely grasp the future which Prince Eric had made possible. I didn't know what to think or how to feel. By the Tides, this future was nothing I'd ever considered. I'd never known it might be like this, and yet it was everything I didn't know I wanted.

"Wait!" Detritus surged forward from the retreating crowd of mer-eel dignitaries and Sharkanian escorts. He looked at me, for once his expression serious with concern. "Promise me you'll take care of them. That you love them."

Mako snorted his disdain, and under normal circumstances I would have done the same. But not this time. Because Ditritus had asked a question I never thought I'd have to answer. Not that long ago, I boasted an empty life filled with annoying requests from mers I couldn't be bothered to know. Now, I apparently had a new job at the palace. And more importantly, my life was filled with two beautiful mer-eels who I wanted in my life in all ways and for always.

I brought their faces to mine. "Yes, I promise to take care of them. Yes, I love them. They are my eel-maids. My ladies. My… my *poopsies*."

My poopsies squealed in delight and wrapped themselves around my hungry tentacles, their arms banding me and their mouths on mine, the nearby audience of the mer-eel delegation, Sharkanian escort, and Altantian royalty completely forgotten.

Minutes—hours?—later, Flottie and Jettie pulled their lips from mine, bodies quivering with desire. A glance around proved we were alone now, and could allow our passion to overtake us, but I still didn't like the idea of fucking where any passing mer could see. I wasn't modest, but was oddly overprotective of my poopsies. Perhaps that emotion would temper with time, but it raged at the moment.

So, when I saw a flash of movement, my tentacles whipped the girls behind me as I faced off with the potential danger, the webbing of my front tentacles belling out and my skin turning a prickly shade of warning yellow.

It was the mermaid from before. The mermaid who no longer held my love lotion shell. Before I could calm my tentacles and inquire about her presence, she spoke. "So did it work? Did they come?"

That made no sense. "Did what work? Did who come?"

"Prince Eric and Princess Ariel." She clasped her hands at her front, the motion wafting a familiar oyster aroma my way. "When the mer-eels arrived, I thought there might be trouble, so I swam away to find Prince Eric. And he sent me to get Officer Mako. If you're here and the mer-eels are gone, does that mean it worked?"

This mermaid was the reason I was married and my eel-maids were safe and didn't have to be fugitives anymore? That strange sensation of gratitude welled inside me again. Guess I'd have to get used to it, since more mers were going to be integral parts of my life going forward. I couldn't be a crabby, crusty outlier anymore.

So I smiled—*smiled!*—at the mermaid and nodded. "Yes, it worked. Thank you for doing that. Otherwise I don't know what might have happened."

A certain mer-eel king would have lost his head, that was for certain.

She waved away my thanks. "It was the least I could do after saying those horrible things about your eel-maids. They aren't trash, Mr. Sea Witch. Especially not if you can love them like you do. They're treasures."

Flottie and Jettie wrapped around me tighter at the compliment and buried their faces in my back. The three of us would have to get used to praise, it seemed.

Murmurs sounded all around us, past the perimeter of my poopsies and the mermaid. I looked around, surprised at the number of mers surrounding us, holding sticks and knives and other hastily-made weapons. Where had they been hiding all this time? And why were they prepared for battle?

"Why are you all here?" I asked, suspicion darkening my voice. I'd nearly killed Detritus to keep my eel-maids safe, and I'd willingly take on this mob for the same reason, although there was little doubt that I would lose.

"We heard you were in trouble, Mr. Sea Witch." Some mer answered. "We came to help."

Another voice from the other side of the mob added. "Did you really risk your life for the eel-maids?"

"Are they really your wives?" Another asked.

"That's so romantic." Yet another voice interjected.

Then they all spoke at once, bombarding me with questions and declarations of support and even the random *it's the least we could do for you.* Before I became too overwhelmed with being at the center of all this enthusiastic attention, Flottie slipped in front of me, her arms spread to the side as if to protect me, and addressed our audience. "Thank you all for your support. Ursule absolutely deserves every bit of it, if you don't mind us saying so." A rumble of good humor followed. "But it's also overwhelming. And, well, we'd like some privacy because, um, we're still… celebrating our marriage, you know, to one another."

By the end, Flottie's voice had softened to nearly a whisper and she fidgeted unconsciously with the tentacles that caressed her in support. Embarrassed as she might have been by her outburst, every mer hung on her words.

"See? I told you. That's so romantic." A voice repeated, prompting good-natured laughter as the mob dissipated, many mers nodding their respects to my poopsies and me. By the time most had returned to their lives, I was numb from too much social interaction. All I wanted was to return to my den with my poopsies and quietly celebrate all the good news of the day.

Well, maybe not too quietly.

"So, you're the one who helped save Mr. Sea Witch?"

A strange merman's voice approached. We all turned to see a young, handsome mer staring at the mermaid with awe and admiration. I turned to the mermaid, who had flushed to a deep pink and blinked dumbly in response.

Laughter bubbled up my throat, even though I managed to swallow it back. This must be the love interest the lotion was intended to attract. Apparently, bravery was far more interesting than food-flavored lotion. Before I could respond on the mermaid's behalf—since she floated there, her mouth opening and closing but no words coming out—Jettie spoke up. "Yes, she's the one who saved Ursule. If she hadn't thought and acted so quickly, Prince Eric wouldn't have arrived in time to keep Ursule from killing the mer-eel king."

"You're very brave." The merman nodded to acknowledge Jettie's declaration, but his attention focused entirely on the mermaid. He grasped her hand in his and held it to his heart. I wasn't an expert, but there seemed to be a particular glimmer of interest in his eyes. "And you smell wonderful."

I turned away before I ruined the budding attraction with triumphant laughter, and urged my poopsies toward our home—

our home!—by way of the kelp forest. After the last several days, we needed a fresh batch of bedding. And dinner.

Flottie and Jettie both danced around me as we hurried on our way, laughing and chatting. Once we arrived at the kelp forest, Jettie's tail gently caressed my jawline as she passed in front of me. "Ursule, can we always be like this?"

"Yes, we can always be searching for fluffy bedding and food." I smirked at my answer.

"And sex!" Jettie added on a celebratory laugh.

Jettie and Flottie both swirled up and around me, their luscious bodies brushing and rubbing mine as desire erupted in my veins. My tentacles caught them and tugged them deeper into the kelp forest with me. Their screams of delight quickly turned to moans of need as I worked them with my mouth, tentacles, and hands.

Flottie ran her fingers through my hair as I lapped at her slick anemone, her throaty voice as languid a caress as Jettie's tail. "Ursule, she means can we always be this happy. This complete. Can we always be together?"

I paused as emotion welled up inside me like a storm surge. I might not be a miracle worker, but I would devote my life to making these two eel-maids happy. "Yes, my poopsies. We'll be together. Forever."

∾

PART OF HIS WORLD

Prince Eric wasn't always royalty. For that matter, he wasn't always a merman.

I stared into the roiling, boiling depths of the hydrothermal vent. Over the past several years, I'd spent countless hours right here, gazing into that churning void. A hopeless man contemplating the darkness of his life before jumping off a bridge or high-rise building.

Only, those options for ending my life weren't available to me. I couldn't take a leap and let gravity do the heavy lifting. Er, dropping. No, if I truly wanted to end my life, I would have to swim with all my might into that bubbling crevice, fighting the upward flow of toxic chemicals choking me until I was boiled alive in the bajillion-degree water surrounding the molten lava. And, if that didn't work, I'd have to suffer being the agonizing poaching until I reached the magma and hopefully sear enough of my body against it that I went into shock and my organs failed, ultimately leading to my death.

Sounded rather unpleasant.

Even in my most despondent moments, I couldn't muster the drive to follow through with it.

So, I had merely gazed, much like I did right now. Bright red magma from deep within the core of this world seeped through the crust to clash with the relatively colder seawater, percolating a cocktail of chemical reactions.

There was more nuance to a hydrothermal vent, but this was where my formal education on chemistry and oceanic biology stopped. I was a community manager by training and trade; my marketable skills were keeping Aquata Prime's luxury floating homes buoyant and the residents of the Lake Triton community happy. I fixed leaking air bladders, unclogged errant seaweed from pipes, orchestrated supply deliveries, and fielded all manner of requests and complaints. Your wine cellar isn't chilling? I'll repair it. You need valet service for your upcoming hydroponic garden party? I'll arrange it. Your house was painted Shortbread Yellow when you specifically asked for Sugar Cookie? I'll get it repainted.

That was when I lived on Aquata Prime. Then, I'd fallen into a mysterious portal which brought me here to the water world of Atlantia.

And turned me into a merman.

Instantly ripped from my homeworld, my family, and my friends, and appearing into this world unknown to me. Everything a mystery. Everyone a stranger. No way back. I'd spent as many years searching for that magic portal as I'd spent contemplating just ending my life. Even when the Atlantian ambassadors cautiously approached me to offer me a job, I'd only accepted because it was something to do that didn't send me into a spiral of depression.

A bedroom at the palace and a personal chef were job perks I hadn't anticipated, but was ever-grateful to have. Someone born in this world wouldn't blink at the constant need to forage for shelter and food, and to avoid becoming someone else's food. But Aquata Prime had a robust economic foundation that cultivated—

I flicked my tail to sluice away from the vent. It didn't matter what Aquata Prime did or did not have. It didn't matter that it had reached the higher levels of the hierarchy of needs, or that Atlantia still circled the bottom levels. Aquata Prime wasn't my home anymore. Never would be, because I'd searched these past years for any clue or hint of evidence of a magical portal. Surely, it was a two-way street and all I needed to do was find the mysterious portal to return home. But that had proved as fruitless as finding any evidence of land above the water's surface of this world.

There wasn't a single myth, fable, or bedtime story about any mystic portal.

"Your Majesty." A pair of rays dipped their heads down in a respective bow as I passed. "May the waters always be warm, Prince Eric."

"And may the currents always be at your back." I returned their greeting with a smile and a royal wave.

The most bizarre part of the whole tumble-into-a-water-world situation—yeah, *more* bizarre than mystic portals and instant conversion to a merman—was the actual job the palace ambassadors had offered me: King.

They'd asked me to be their king. King of their entire freaking world. Sure, I'd managed one of Aquata Prime's largest lake communities, but *King of the Planet* was a big step up in pay grade. And in responsibility. I had almost declined because I could barely take care of myself in this new world, let alone make the kinds of decisions that would impact millions of creatures.

The real Atlantian King had died years before, supposedly in a skirmish against the Sharkanians, although I'd never found anyone who had been there to witness it. Not that I looked too hard. I admittedly only cared to the extent the answer might impact my own mortality. Otherwise, *how* the former king had bit it didn't really matter. Whether he'd died of natural causes, had been killed honorably, or had been stabbed in the back, the result was the same. His absence left a turbulent wake that buffeted all of Atlantia.

And they needed me to calm those churning waters.

A part of me wanted to decline, and continue my hopeless yearning for a different life. Another other part of me realized maybe this offer was the *different life* I yearned for. Yet another, smaller, part of me knew such a monumental commitment would focus my energies away from my many morose thoughts. So, I accepted, asked them to just consider me Prince Eric instead of King Eric, and stopped looking for the portal and possible ways to die. I looked toward the future of Atlantia and how I could bring peace, harmony, and a sense of purpose to the land. Er, water.

"I want to be the Princess!" A child's voice sounded from over a small knoll.

I drifted toward it out of curiosity and was delighted to find a small group of mer-children playing pretend with crudely-made dolls. One held a bright yellow spear that resembled my trident. Another had pointy shards of shells sewn into the mouth. No doubt representing a Sharkanian, likely General Mako, my recently-appointed Chief Officer of the Law. He and I had an antagonistic past, mostly because he'd assumed I was a war-mongering king like the previous one and I'd assumed he was nothing but a mindless killer.

Funny how we now respected each other enough to work together toward the betterment of all Atlantians.

Okay, maybe not funny so much as interesting. And all due to the gentle guidance and loving influence of the mer represented by the other doll wrapped in green kelp with a bright pink tendril of soft coral drifting from her head. Princess Ariel.

Princess Ariel, who had also fallen through a magic portal between Aquata Prime and Atlantia and turned into a mermaid. A beautiful, funny, kind, passionate mermaid. I'd instantly fallen in love with her.

Wellll, not *instantly*. A sacred room in the palace had a mosaic of a mermaid who looked exactly like Ariel… which was saying something because we didn't look like typical mers. Mers who were born on Atlantia had wider-set eyes and flatter mouths, somewhat resembling the fish of Aquata Prime. By contrast, Ariel and I had rounder faces, our eyes set closer and facing more forward. We also had the mutual aversion to public fornication which the Atlantians lacked. Getting used to the fact that most mers and other aquatic creatures fucked whenever, wherever, and with whomever they felt like had taken some time.

Since I hadn't been fucking anyone, I'd spent most of my rare off-duty time in that room, staring at the image of the beautiful mer with brilliant pink hair, emerald green tail, luscious curves, and come-hither smirk. Yes, I'd spent years dreaming up countless interactions with the image, wishing she was real, falling in love with her—or at least with my imagined portrayal of her—and desiring her. Until one day she appeared in my palace, in the flesh.

And more amazing that anything I'd envisioned.

Much to my surprise, and delight, she'd spent time staring at an image of me on Aquata Prime, similarly falling in love. Best of all, the real me hadn't disappointed. She still loved me.

"Grrr, Prince Eric. I will fight you for Princess Ariel's love."

The mer-child with the Mako doll growled. I bit my lips to keep from laughing; his impersonation of the Sharkanian was spot-on.

"Step aside, chum." The one holding the doll with the trident said. I pursed my lips at his weird inflections. I sounded nothing like that. "Princess Ariel belongs to me."

Okay, I never said that.

The mer-child continued. "She loves my long, thick trident, and you don't have one."

I clamped my hands over my mouth as my heart sank. Yes, I'd actually said that. In jest. In what I thought had been a private corner with no one listening to my teasing come-on to Ariel. It had been a joke, and Ariel had laughed as I'd expected, but now it just sounded creepy, especially spoken by a child. I'd have to be even more vigilant about what I said outside of our bedroom.

"Step aside you two, Princess Ariel is in love with me!" A fourth mer-child with a doll that trailed several wriggling strands of kelp, two of which were wrapped around slender reeds— obviously Ursule the Sea Witch and his two eel-maid *poopsies* who never left his side—"And I will zap you with my magic to prove it!"

Um, Ursule didn't actually have any *magic*. But who was I to ruin a good show?

"I don't love any of you." Princess Ariel doll wagged between the other three dolls, her hand on her hip in a stance that was surprisingly accurate. The mer-child spoke in an irritated huff. "And I'm perfectly capable of defending myself. Take that!"

I watched in a mixture of horror and humor as the Princess Ariel doll battled and easily defeated the other three dolls in a spectacular display of water aerobatics and deadly force.

As the Princess Ariel doll huffed her victory cheer, I drifted over the mound toward the mer-children.

"Princess Ariel is amazing!" I declared. The mer-children startled at my voice, and quickly bowed. I continued, addressing the mer-child with the Ariel doll. "I know she can take care of herself, but do you think Ariel will find it in her heart to fall in love with me?"

"Will you bring her sea flowers?" The little mermaid giggled. When I nodded enthusiastically, she smiled. "Okay, Your Majesty. She can fall in love with you. But only because you're very nice. And handsome."

Glad to know those were my winning qualities.

"That makes me very happy—"

"Sorry for the interruption, Prince Eric." Mako's voice sounded from behind me. "But you're going to be late for your wedding."

I whirled around, my heart in my throat. Damn, I'd lost track of time! Today was my wedding day. I was marrying Ariel—yep, she'd found it in her heart to fall in love with me—and the excitement beating in my chest had nearly driven me out of my scales. I'd needed some time alone. Time to contemplate the path either Fate or Chance had set before me. Time to say good-bye to the dark past that had nearly been my end. To give thanks for the choices I'd made and hadn't made, all which had led up to today. The day I was marrying an amazing woman.

That is, if I didn't miss the whole thing because I'd taken a morning swim to calm my nerves and apparently wandered too far into contemplating-my-life territory.

"Children, enjoy your play." I said quickly to the mer-children who were already back to their dolls. "Let's make haste, Mako. I wouldn't miss this occasion for all the water in the world."

He turned to escort me to the palace, but we had not traveled far when we were brought up short by a shimmery image before us. A long slash surrounded by radiating ripples of water floated there. I hadn't seen it before when I'd been distracted by the children's play. Nothing around us should be creating the odd ripples, their surface nearly reflective like a funhouse mirror. The slash relaxed, widening, and an image appeared. A moving image asynchronous with the ocean floor around us. Bright colors passed, images taking shape, focusing until I realized what I saw.

People.

People with legs who walked on a carpeted floor. The large entertaining room of a lake house, much like those floating on Aquata Prime's Lake Triton.

My home.

After all these years, I finally found the mystic portal. Or maybe it had found me. Whichever the case, it meant I could return to my home, my family, my friends. I could return to the life I'd known. I could stop pretending I was anything more than merely a community manager. And, because there was apparently a time differential between the two worlds, my years spent here equated to only a few months missing from Aquata Prime. Returning would be almost seamless.

Yearning bloomed in my chest.

But not yearning for the life in front of me, the possible life this portal dangled like a carrot with shimmering edges. I yearned for the pink-haired mermaid who was at this moment preparing to bind herself to me for the rest of our lives. The woman who would swim at my side and work tirelessly to make Atlantia the best possible world for its inhabitants.

The life beyond the rippling portal didn't entice me. The promise of going back to my former life didn't matter. I yearned for the life we were making right here.

"What is that, Your Majesty?" Mako floated quietly beside me, but he was tensed for battle. "Who are those strange mers with two tails?"

Mako knew Ariel and I were not originally from this world, but I'd never elaborated on what our homeworld was like. He might enjoy the stories, but today—right now—was not the time for it.

I clamped a hand on his shoulder and steered him away. "It's a portal between our worlds, like what brought Ariel and me here. Send someone to guard it in case someone falls through or an Atlantian gets too close. I'll tell you more about it later, but not today. Not now. We have a wedding to attend, and I have a beautiful mermaid to marry."

Mako, being the trustworthy Officer I knew he was, merely nodded his understanding. And, without another word, we sluiced away from the portal and toward the palace. Toward my wedding. My bride. The love of my life. And our future together. She was part of my world, now. And our world was Atlantia.

ABOUT AVA

Ava Cuvay is an award-winning bestselling author of out of this world Sci-fi and Paranormal Romance featuring sassy heroines, gutsy heroes, passion, adventure… and the word "moist".

She resides in central Indiana with her own scruffy-looking nerfherder and teen kiddos who think her "Rizz" is "cringe" but she "passes the vibe check" and her books "hit different." No cap.

She believes life is too short to bother with negative people, everything is better with Champagne, and Han Solo shot first. Star Wars references are her love language.

SIGN UP FOR AN EXCLUSIVE BONUS SCENE AND MORE BOOK NEWS!

Join my newsletter for an exclusive bonus scene, freebies, Advanced Reader Copy opportunities, and fun info! https://drinkingthestarspressllc.eo.page/n9r2d

PLEASE LEAVE A REVIEW!

Book reviews are one of the few ways we authors receive feedback from our readers. And we hunger for it! Please take a few minutes and leave a review this book. Thank you!